The Britwhistles Win a Prize

The Britwhistles Win a Prize

Written and Illustrated by

Wendy Hamilton

ZealAus Publishing

The Britwhistles Win a Prize

This is a revised edition

ISBN: 978-1-925888-71-3 (e)
ISBN: 978-1-925888-72-0 (hc)
ISBN: 978-1-925888-73-7 (sc)

This book is dedicated
to my daughter

Ruth Hamilton.

Who convinced me
I could illustrate.

Contents

The Britwhistles lived at Toot Cottage.

Wendy Hamilton

New Neighbors

It was a still day and the smoke coming from the chimney of a wooden house with a deep veranda drifted up lazily. The back door opened and a small elderly woman hobbled down the steps and over to a woodshed propped against a bigger shed.

"What are you doing, Alfred?" she said, leaning back and staring up at an elderly man on a ladder.

"I'm putting a windmill on the workshop. This is the best spot to catch the wind."

"I can see that, I'm talking about the reindeer antlers your wearing. Christmas is a long way off."

"These?" Alfred adjusted the headband on his bald head.

"Of course I mean those!"

"I'm just having fun with our new neighbour."

The Britwhistles Win a Prize

Myrtle shifted her gaze to the brick house over the fence. "What do you mean? We have been here for two weeks and not laid eyes on our neighbour."

"We may not have laid eyes on the neighbour, but trust me, the neighbour is watching, always watching."

"Oh Alfred, how can you say such a thing?"

"Look at the window opposite us."

"I'm looking."

"Right at the bottom of the curtain you will see two black rings."

Myrtle slid her glasses down her nose a little and peered over the top of the rims.

"Do you see them?"

"I think so, I saw something at the bottom of the curtain, but whatever it was, it's gone now."

Alfred continued screwing the windmill to the roof of the shed. "Those, my dear, are binoculars."

Myrtle hastily smoothed the apron around her waist and tucked a stray of grey hair into the bun on the top of her head. "Oh Alfred, I don't like the feeling of being on show. What an awful neighbour. Do you think we have done the wrong thing buying this house?"

Alfred took a screw out of his pocket and slotted it into a hole in the windmill's frame.

"Don't be silly, Myrtle," he said, twisting his

screwdriver vigorously, "we have waited a long time to find a place like this. It's hard to find a house with an orchard and woodstove these days."

Myrtle thought about the big black range in the kitchen and smiled. "It bakes beautifully, and the garden is perfect for the grandchildren. I guess a nosy neighbour is a small price to pay."

"It will be fun; I love a sneaky nosy neighbour. I hope to have the doorbell on before she comes calling."

The smile disappeared from Myrtle's face and she put her hands on her hips. "You are not to put the whistle on the front door of this house, Alfred."

Alfred's vigorous arm movements stopped.

"But I made it myself and the new house won't feel like home without it," he said, in a peeved tone.

"I don't care."

The ladder wobbled as Alfred swivelled to look at Myrtle better.

"Watch out," shouted Myrtle, clutching the sides of it, "you'll fall if you are not careful."

Alfred poked his head through the rungs and looked down at his wife. "What is the point of having a name like Britwhistle if I can't have a whistle instead of a doorbell? Besides," he added mischievously, "it's lots of fun."

Myrtle twisted her head around the side of the

ladder and looked up at her husband with a stern face. "Now that is exactly the attitude that I am afraid of, Alfred Henry. You are too old for all these pranks. Remember what happened at the last house?"

"It is only a little whistle."

"It is not a little whistle. It is a great whopping train whistle as you well know. And it is not nice how you unleash that hideous shriek on people when they least expect it. You are not to put it on the door of this house. We're new in the area. I want to make friends not enemies."

"It's only a bit of fun."

"It might be for you... and occasionally a few others," admitted Myrtle, suppressing a smile, "but it is the sort of fun that ends in tears. Remember the lady who fell off the porch?"

Alfred's shoulders stumped. He felt bad about that incident as he was a very kind old man. "What if I promise not to pull the string when people aren't looking?"

Myrtle's face and voice softened.

"No, Dear, a noise like that is disastrous for a person with a weak bladder. I don't want another vicar embarrassed like the last one. It was lucky your trousers fitted him; we had to give a big donation for the church organ to make up for that."

Alfred sighed deeply, and even the bells on the antlers seemed to droop. "I still say, anyone with a name like Britwhistle ought to have a whistle instead of a doorbell," he said in a small voice.

"I'll tell you what, Alfie, how about a compromise? We will call the house Toot Cottage and you can mount your whistle out here on the side of the shed. You make such a noise in your workshop I need something loud to get your attention."

It was suddenly very silent in the garden; the only sound was the purring of an enormous orange cat who was rubbing himself around Myrtle's legs. At last, Alfred spoke. "Oh, alright."

Myrtle beamed. "Good on you, Dear, I know that wasn't easy."

Alfred picked up his screwdriver and turned his attention back to his windmill while Myrtle's thoughts shifted to the window opposite them. The black rings were at the bottom of the curtain once again.

"Alfie, will we ever meet the neighbour face to face?"

"Sure we will, curiosity will drive her to our door."

"You seem very certain the neighbour is a woman."

"Don't you remember the Real Estate Agent told

us the only neighbour was the woman next door."

Myrtle tickled the cat's head. "Oh, that's right," she said, remembering the conversation. "If she is nosy enough to spy on us, I suppose she will want to see what our furniture is like."

Alfred gave a final twist to the last screw and wriggled the windmill to make sure it was firm. "She already knows that!" he said, climbing down the ladder. "I saw her watching from behind the curtain in the front room when the men were unloading the removal truck. But she will want to know where you put everything, and that is hard to do from behind a curtain."

Myrtle looked down the garden path at the small tin shed in the distance and giggled. "I wonder what she thought the composting toilet was?"

Alfred, reaching the bottom of the ladder, gave a snort of laughter. "And all my tools and laboratory equipment." His eyes gleamed. "I shall tell her I am building a nuclear power station."

Myrtle gave her husband a friendly little punch on the shoulder. "You're a naughty man."

Alfred's face radiated innocence as he opened his blue eyes wide. "I have no idea what you are talking about, Myrtle."

"Oh yes you do," she chuckled.

The cat yawned and stretched.

"Do you think Marmaduke should be outside?" said Alfred, stroking the enormous cat. "We don't want to lose him."

"I think so," said Myrtle, "I've buttered his paws and the vet said two weeks was long enough to keep him inside."

While they watched the cat wandered over to a nearby tree, sniffed the trunk, and sprayed the surrounding grass.

"I expect he wants to mark out his territory," said Alfred. He looked at the cat with pride. "I wouldn't like to be a cat and come up against Marmaduke."

Myrtle frowned as she bent over and picked up an armful of firewood. "I hope the neighbour doesn't have a cat, if Marmaduke bashes it up we will be in trouble."

Alfred took the antlers off and while his wife's back was still turned, popped them on her head. "You worry too much, Myrtle Turtle, the neighbour does not have a cat."

But he was wrong; the neighbour did have a cat.

Cat Troubles

Nelly brushed the long fur of her fluffy white cat. "One more week, Snowball, and we will have another trophy for the china cabinet. You're sure to win best cat of the show again."

A loud meow coming from over the fence caught her attention. Stiffening, she put the brush down and went over to the window. Snowball had also heard the meow. He stalked across the kitchen floor as Nelly picked up her binoculars.

"I hope that weird couple next door don't have a cat," she muttered, as she tweaked the bottom of the curtain up and gazed over the fence. What she saw made her suck in her breath sharply, for not more than a few yards away the most enormous cat she had ever seen was marking out his territory.

"That's a huge brute," she exclaimed. "I don't like the look of him. Stay away from that big orange beast, my precious." Nelly turned her head to look at Snowball, but he had disappeared.

"Snowball, here, puss, puss," she called, as she searched through the house.

A gust of wind blew and a door banged. Nelly's head whipped around and her hand flew to her mouth when she saw that the backdoor had blown open.

"Snowball, here, puss, puss, puss," she called, frantically running to the door. She was just in time to hear a dreadful rumpus of spitting, and snarling, and yowling, and minutes later, Snowball streaked into the house and hid behind the couch.

It took half a tin of fish to coax him into the open, but as soon as Nelly saw him close up all her hopes for winning a trophy were dashed. She picked up her howling cat and, quivering with anger, marched down the Britwhistle's front path and onto the veranda. Holding the cat under one arm, she jangled the chain of the brass bell by the door. Myrtle, opening the door, saw a thin woman wearing a striped rugby shirt confronting her.

"Hello, what can I do for you?" she said, taking a step backwards.

Nelly's eyes flew open and she gazed at the top

of Myrtle's head.

Myrtle, suddenly remembering the antlers, dragged them off and threw them onto a nearby chair. "What is the trouble?" she said, smoothing her hair.

"This is the trouble," spat Nelly, sticking out her chin. "Your cat did this." She turned her cat around and showed Myrtle the large bald patch on his side.

Myrtle's face crumpled into dismay. "Oh dear, I'm so sorry. We will pay the vet's bill."

"I don't need a vet, it's not that bad, it's a miracle I need. The cat show is next week and I can't enter him looking like this!"

Myrtle opened the door wide and smiled nervously. "I'm Myrtle and I have been wanting to meet you. Come in and have a cup of tea, my husband, Alfred, is a scientist and inventor, he might be able to make a fur growing potion."

Nelly's chin dropped and her voice became less aggressive. "I'm, Nelly, and this is my cat, Snowball," she said, as she followed Myrtle through the front room to the cosy kitchen behind.

Myrtle slid the kettle on the back of the stove to the spot over the fire-box. "Take a seat," she said, pulling a chair out from the kitchen table, "I'll get my husband." As Nelly sat down, Myrtle opened the back door and bashed a gong mounted on the wall outside the door. "He'll be here in a minute, he's in his workshop," she said, coming inside again and taking a cake out of the oven. "Do you like your tea, weak or strong, Nelly?"

"Strong."

Alfred arrived by the time the tea was made and the cake cut. He strode into the room looking happy because he smelt chocolate cake. When he saw Nelly, he halted and his eyes flew open in surprise.

"This is Nelly, our neighbour," said Myrtle. She shot him a 'be-nice,' look. "Marmaduke and Snowball have had a fight."

"Did Marmaduke win?" said Alfred, with the air of a coach inquiring after his prize-fighter.

Myrtle gave him a sharp nudge as Nelly, scowling, showed Alfred the big bald patch.

"Your cat is a bully and a menace."

Alfred hid his pride in Marmaduke's handiwork by coughing into his elbow.

"Alfred, Dear," Myrtle plucked at his sleeve to get his attention, "as you are so clever, perhaps you can invent something to fix the problem."

Alfred stopped coughing and scratched his head. Then he took a measuring tape and a notebook from his back pocket. "Let me have a closer look at the bald spot," he said, taking a pencil from behind his ear. Nelly stretched the cat around once more, and

The Britwhistles Win a Prize

Alfred (his face straight and serious) measured the mangy part several times. Then he rubbed the white fur between his fingers and wrote numbers down in his notebook. Myrtle, leaning over his shoulder felt hopeful, and Nelly, noticing Myrtle's faith in her husband, starting to think the cat show was not impossible after all. When Alfred had enough information he wound up the tape measure and put the pencil behind his ear. Myrtle bit her fingernails and looked at him anxiously.

"Can you do something, Alfred?"

"I think so," said Alfred, staring hard at the numbers on his page. "I won't be long." With that, he turned on his heel, but instead of marching out to his workshop (as his wife expected) he strode through the front room and into the bedroom.

Myrtle's face relaxed as she turned to Nelly. "I knew he could fix Snowball. My husband is a very clever man. Would you like another slice of cake, Nelly, while he concocts something?"

Nelly nodded and passed her empty plate to Myrtle. While they waited for Alfred to produce a miracle, Myrtle and Nelly got to know each other a little. Although the introduction had started badly things improved as the visit went on. Nelly got to satisfy her curiosity about the house, and Myrtle learnt much about the town and the people because

Nelly was a gossip.

"If you want anything, go to Molly's Emporium," she said, taking a sip of tea. "She sells everything, although she has far too much silly stuff for children because she had ten of her own."

"Ten," said Myrtle faintly.

"Yes, seven boys and three girls, and the boys were right brats, always playing pranks." Nelly pointed at the big woodstove under the mantelpiece. "When are you going to get a new stove?"

"Oh, I'm not, Alfred and I want to live off the grid."

"What does that mean?" Nelly stroked Snowball absentmindedly while she spoke.

"We don't want to use electricity," said Myrtle.

Nelly's hand stopped at the end of a stroke and hung suspended in the air. "Not use electricity! Everyone uses electricity."

"Alfred wants to use alternate energy."

Nelly's eyes narrowed suspiciously. "You're not going to use some new fandangle rays, are you? I don't want them leaking over to my place and giving me cancer."

"No, nothing like that, just a windmill, generator, and of course, the woodstove."

Nelly sniffed and resumed stroking Snowball. "Each to their own. I suppose he will join the Men's

The Britwhistles Win a Prize

Shed that meets at Ron Cathcart's on Thursdays; they are into that sort of stuff, or rather, they say they are," Nelly gave another sniff, "but if you ask me, I think they go because Ron's wife is a marvellous cook. She runs the Weight Watchers club." Nelly eyed Myrtle's waistline. "I can give you her phone number if you want to join. They are not picky about members. If you are fat, you're invited."

"Does Molly sell fabric?" asked Myrtle, wincing at the sharp words.

"Oh yes, she's got oodles of the stuff. What do you want it for?"

"I've decided to take up patchwork quilting," said Myrtle.

Nelly looked at Myrtle as if she couldn't have heard correctly. "Why would you bother cutting fabric into little squares only to sew them all back together again?"

"Because I want to make something special."

"Your mad to do it, but if that's the case, the patchwork club meets at Mrs Grundy's place every Wednesday." Nelly sniffed, "they might accept you, it all depends on Mrs Grundy. But don't wear anything strange." She glanced through the kitchen door at the antlers in the other room. "And watch out for Edna…"

Myrtle squirmed uncomfortably.

"She used to be in charge of…"

Alfred strode into the room, cutting Nelly's speech short. Both women looked at him expectantly.

Myrtle, looking at her husband's face, beamed. "You did invent something, what is it? I can see you're hiding something behind your back."

"I certainly did."

With that, Alfred whisked his hand out with a flourish. A small circle of brown fur on a loop of wide elastic dangled from his fingers.

Myrtle's face crumpled into dismay. "Oh Alfred, you can do better than that, I expected you to make some kind of fur-growing ointment."

Alfred's eyebrows jutted out and he scowled. "It's the best I can do without my lab fully set up. This will work. The band wraps around the cat's stomach and holds the fur in place."

Nelly, who had been silent with disappointment, suddenly found her voice.

"That dreadful thing will not fool the judges. It is not even white or real. It looks like brown rabbit fur."

"Brown rabbit!" Myrtle snatched the patch from Alfred's hand and peered at it suspiciously. "Just where did you get this fur, Alfred?"

Alfred looked uncomfortable and gave a hollow cough. "From the closet."

The Britwhistles Win a Prize

"Alfred! Did you use my good Sunday coat?"

The room felt suddenly chilly to Alfred as two hostile women glared at him. He ran his finger around the inside of his shirt collar. "I might have."

"Alfred Henry Britwhistle!"

"Well, of all the nerve!" said Nelly, hitching Snowball under her arm and standing up. "You will hear from my lawyer about this Alfred Britwhistle." With that, she stomped out of the house, slamming the door behind her.

Myrtle, following closely behind, veered off into the bedroom and opened the door of the big wooden closet in the room's corner. She fished about inside it and pulled out a coat with a large hole in it. "Oh, Alfred!" she said in dismay, "right in the middle of the front. You could have at least taken it closer to the hem, I might have been able to salvage it if you had."

Alfred's shoulders drooped and he looked downcast for a moment. "Sorry Myrtle, I wasn't thinking. He plopped his invention on top of his bald head and slipped the elastic under his chin. It sat there like a tiny hat as he absent-mindedly plucked the elastic strap with his finger. It made a pleasing thwack as it hit his skin. A slow smile spread over his face as he plucked the elastic to the rhythm of an old nursery rhyme.

"Pussy cat, pussy cat, where have you been?" he chanted softly.

"I've been to London to visit the Queen."

"Stop that, you silly man." Myrtle's voice was grim and she spoke through thin lips.

But Alfred, who knew his wife well, saw the corners of her mouth turn up the tiniest bit. So instead of stopping, he said with a twinkle in his eye, "listen to this Myrtle-Turtle, I've made up a good one."

"Pussy cat, pussy cat, why aren't you clean?"

"I've been in a fight; I'm not fit to be seen."

And now Myrtle's mouth really did curl up and she even laughed. Although she pretended it was a snort. "Do you really think we will get a letter from her lawyer?" she said, putting her coat in the furthest corner of the wardrobe.

Underneath all his playfulness Alfred was a shrewd judge of character. "Nah, that type is all bluff. She probably doesn't even know a lawyer."

"I hope you're right," said Myrtle with a sigh, as she shut the door and turned the little key in the lock."

Molly's Emporium

Myrtle picked the antlers off the wingback chair where they had fallen. "Oh Alfred," she said with a chuckle, "I hate to think what Nelly will say about us? I forgot these goofy things were sitting on my head and I was wearing them when I answered the door."

Alfred gave a shout of laughter. "Sneaking them on your head while your arms were full was a good move, but I never expected it to be that good."

Myrtle grinned and threw the antlers at him before sitting down and taking up her knitting. Alfred caught them and sat in a chair opposite her. "At least the visit wasn't a total disaster," she said, "Nelly told me about a patchwork club that meets

18

on Wednesdays. There is a Men's Shed around here too, and apparently they mess around with alternate energy, although Nelly was sure they only went there because of the wonderful lunch."

Alfred stretched out his legs and wiggled his toes. "I like the sound of that club."

Myrtle, knitting a few more stitches, noticed she was running out of wool. "And there is a shop in town called Molly's Emporium." The knitting needles paused as she gazed upwards. "Nelly said something weird, what was it?" she stroked her chin gently with the empty needle. "That's right," her eyes dropped and she looked at Alfred, "she said the shop sold lots of silly stuff because Molly raised ten children, seven of them boys."

"Silly stuff for boys!" Alfred drew his legs in and sat up straight. "I like the sound of that. Let's go shopping."

"Not now, Alfred, it's getting late and I have got to start dinner." Myrtle put her needles together and rolled her knitting around them. "Well go tomorrow as soon as we finish the chores."

"Alright," said Alfred, looking pleased. "I'll chop the wood now, that will hurry things up a bit."

With that, Myrtle went to make dinner and Alfred chopped a big pile of kindling. Early next morning, Alfred put on his hat and Myrtle picked up her shopping basket. Then they locked the door and put the key under the doormat. After walking a short distance, they came across a corner store with 'Molly's Emporium' written on the window.

"This must be it," said Alfred. A little bell tinkled as he pushed the door open.

"It must be," said Myrtle, following him in.

A woman with fizzy hair and a spreading figure stood behind the counter. She was the 'Molly,' bit of the sign. The 'Emporium,' lay over shelves, hung off racks, and oozed out of nooks and crannies. Behind Molly was a wall of brightly coloured sweets in glass jars.

Alfred's eyes grew wide with childlike wonder as he gazed at them. "This must be the silly stuff Nelly talked about."

Molly smiled, "no, she means Boy's Corner." She pointed to a nearby aisle. "It's down aisle three."

For a man like Alfred, Boy's Corner was a treasure. There were fake spiders, latex vomit, stink bombs, and toothpaste to turn teeth green, as well as, non-lathering soap, sneezing powder, and rubber snakes. In addition, there were chemistry sets, magic tricks, and much more. While Myrtle bought a ball of wool and fingered the fabric, Alfred made a list of the pranks he planned to play on Nelly. At length, Myrtle was ready to go.

"Have you seen anything you want, Alfie?" she called down the aisle.

"No," fibbed Alfred.

They said goodbye to Molly and started walking home, but at the crossroad where the town petered into the country, Alfred stopped.

"You go on ahead, Myrtle, I think I'll go back. I saw a nice little fishing rod that will be ideal for Peter when the children come for Christmas."

"Alright dear, while you're at it, get a pretty bucket. Sally and I can collect shells while you and Peter are fishing."

"Of course," said Alfred, turning red and running his finger around his collar. He didn't dare tell his wife of the tricks he planned to play on Nelly, because he knew she would not approve. He turned and strode back to the store while Myrtle hobbled on slowly.

Alfred arrived home not long after Myrtle and went straight to his workshop. He was carrying a fishing rod, a red bucket, and a large box. Then he went to find his wife. "I got a bucket for Sally," he said, putting it on the kitchen table, "do you like it?"

"It's wonderful, red is such a cheerful colour and it's got a shell on it. How clever of you, Alfie. Sally will love it." She leaned towards him and gave him a little kiss.

"And see the fishing rod I got for Peter?" Alfred bent the top of it over. "It will take an enormous fish to break this little beauty."

"Oh Alfred, you have been clever, let's put them in the bedrooms now."

Without replying, Alfred bustled over to the staircase in the kitchen's corner and bounced up the steps (taking care that the fishing rod did not hook the picture of Great Aunty Eliza off the wall.)

"Oh, do be careful, Love, don't trip," said Myrtle, picking up the shell bucket, "bones break easily at our age." She put a foot on the first step, gripped the handrail and hoisted herself up.

"Which room is for Peter?" called Alfred, his voice echoing through the empty rooms.

"Either, they are both the same, you choose," said Myrtle, stumping up onto the small landing.

"I fancy this one," said Alfred. He went through the door on the left side of the landing and leaned the fishing rod in the corner.

"That settles it nicely," said Myrtle, going through the opposite door. She sat the bucket in the window alcove. There was thick dust on the floor and the windowsill. "It's awfully grubby in here," shouted Myrtle, drawing her finger across the dirty windowpane.

"And stuffy," Alfred shouted, as he wrenched up the window. A breeze blew in, and the cobwebs dangling from the sloping ceiling wobbled.

"Be a love and pop down for a broom and duster, Alfie."

"Right-oh, do you want me to bring up a bucket of water and a mop too?"

"Only if you can manage it. I don't want you tumbling down the stairs."

"Don't fuss, Woman, I don't need wrapping in cotton wool."

He strode to the landing and was about to sit on the stair rail when Myrtle popped her head out of Sally's room.

"If you slide down the bannister, Alfred Henry Britwhistle, I will not make apple pie tonight."

"You're no fun anymore," grumbled Alfred, stamping down the stairs. "It had better be a big pie," he shouted over his shoulder.

He went into the laundry and while he was filling a bucket with water, glanced through the window and saw Nelly going out her front gate. The opportunity for playing a trick was too good to miss, so Alfred turned off the water, put the bucket down and snuck off to his workshop.

Alfred Plays a Trick

Alfred's secret purchase was hidden in the tool chest under his workbench. He opened the chest and peered into the box from Molly's Emporium. The selection of tricks in there was so magnificent it was hard to choose between them. In the end, he picked out a villainous-looking snake.

"You little beauty," he said, handling it as if it were a real one, "next time the postman comes Nelly will get a big surprise." He crept along the driveway and peered down the road. His neighbour was a dot in the distance, so he slipped the snake into her letterbox.

When Alfred got back to the attic, Myrtle expected him to still be angry with her, but to her surprise he was whistling. "I promise it will be a big one," she said, taking the broom from him.

"What will be big?" said Alfred. In his excitement over the snake, he had forgotten all about their little tiff over the bannister.

"The apple pie, of course," said Myrtle, sweeping cobwebs off the ceiling.

"Oh, the pie, yes that will be nice." His mind was still on the snake. He put down the bucket a little too hard and water slopped over the side and splashed onto the floor. As he mopped it up, he wished Peter and Sally had already come so he had someone to share his secret with. "Do you think Nelly will scream?" he said.

"Why would Nelly scream?" said Myrtle, dropping the end of the broom onto the floor.

Alfred's eyes flew open. He hadn't meant to speak out loud. "Because…" he scanned the room for inspiration, "because…"

"Because why?"

"Because she will be shocked to see the windows of this house clean," finished Alfred in a rush of words.

"I suppose she will," said Myrtle, sweeping down a big cobweb, "they've been dirty for ages."

The scream took a long time to come, but when it came it was loud and shrill. Myrtle, who had just finished polishing the window was pleased.

The Britwhistles Win a Prize

"I thought you were exaggerating when you said Nelly would scream over clean windows, Alfie, but you were quite right. You are such a good judge of character." She leaned out the window and waved at her neighbour. "I hope you enjoyed our little surprise. I'll deal with the ones below this afternoon."

At this Nelly gave another shriek and ran down her driveway.

"That was odd," said Myrtle, "I wonder why she rushed off like that?"

"I think she is worried about snakes under her letterbox," said Alfred, trying not to burst out laughing.

"What a strange woman," said Myrtle, giving a final wipe to the windowsill.

They continued working and by lunchtime the rooms in the attic were spotless.

"We have a lot to do before Christmas," said Myrtle, looking around the bare rooms. "How long do you think it will take you to build the beds?"

"Quite some time," said Alfred vaguely. "They can't be ordinary beds."

"Remember how Peter and Sally liked the pictures in Goldilocks and the Three Bears when they were little," said Myrtle, "perhaps you could make beds like those."

"Splendid idea," said Alfred. "I'll start on them as soon as I get my workshop set up."

"And I shall join the patchwork club and learn to make patchwork quilts."

So early on Wednesday morning, Myrtle baked a cake, and when it was cool, she put it in a cake tin and popped it in her basket. "I've left a meat pie in the fridge for your lunch, Alfie," she said, as she put on her hat. "I'll be away most of the day but I'll be back in time to make dinner." She kissed him. "Have a nice day dear."

Once Myrtle was gone, Alfred rushed into his workshop and dragged the tool chest out from under his workbench. He had discovered (by a bit of spying himself) that Nelly spent most of Wednesday morning watching the soap operas. Alfred was a noisy man by nature but he could be silent when he wanted. Nelly heard nothing as he attached a tiny pulley to her porch and slipped a fishing line around it. The nylon ran in a loop from Nelly's house to a small pulley on Alfred's workshop and was almost invisible.

"She will never see it," said Alfred to Marmaduke, when he had finished. The cat watched lazily as Alfred dipped into his box of tricks. "Beautiful," he said, holding a spider up to the light, "so realistic." He pulled out several more and attached a long string to each of them. Then he tied them to the nylon on his side of the fence. "Let's see how this goes, Marmaduke," said Alfred, pulling the top of the loop towards him. As he pulled, the spiders on the bottom string slid towards Nelly's house a little way. Alfred kept pulling and soon a long line of spiders dangled outside Nelly's back door. He had only got them into position when he heard music coming from Nelly's house, and the sound of the postman's motorbike in the distance.

"Good, 'Where the Heart Churns' is finished," Alfred muttered to himself. "She'll be out to clear the mailbox in a minute." He fixed his gaze on Nelly's back door and soon it opened. Alfred jiggled the fishing line, so the spiders jumped and leapt, but Nelly passed under them without noticing a thing.

"Blow," said Alfred, rubbing his chin. "What went wrong, Marmaduke?"

While Nelly cleared her letterbox, Alfred studied the problem, and by the time she was halfway down her driveway he knew what was wrong. "I didn't allow for the back-door-steps; I should have made the strings a little longer. If only I could get her to jump up."

As if the cat knew what he was saying, Marmaduke looked at the train whistle mounted on the side of the shed.

"The very thing," said Alfred, stooping to stroke him. "How fortunate Myrtle insisted I put it out here." He stretched out his arm and took hold of the whistle-string, while his other hand grasped the nylon line.

"Wait for it, wait for it," he whispered to the cat. "She's almost under them, one, two, three, NOW." He jiggled the line violently as he pulled the whistle-string.

Shrieeeeeeeeeeeeek screamed the whistle.

Eeeeeeeeeeeeeeeek shrieked Nelly. The letters flew out of her hand as she leapt high into the air. It was a magnificent leap, just high enough for the spiders to jump in front of her face and land in her hair. Then there were more shrieks and more leaps.

"Haw haw ha ha," laughed Alfred Henry, slapping his knees and stomping his feet. His face was red with mischief and he looked like he was doing a little dance.

Nelly, hearing the laughter, stopped leaping and looked at the spiders more closely. That was when she saw the fishing line running from her back door. She followed it to the boundary and stood on the bottom rail of the fence. Alfred was standing on the steps of his workshop still laughing when Nelly's irate face popped up over the top of the fence palings. She glared as she shook her fist at him. "I'll get the police onto you Alfred Britwhistle if you do that again," she shouted.

"It's a bit of fun to make up for spying on us," said Alfred, smoothly.

"I did not spy on you," lied Nelly, turning red.

"Yes, you did."

"I did not."

"Well, we can pretend you didn't but we both know that you did," said Alfred.

Nelly gave a snort of rage, jumped down and stomped back to her house.

Alfred waited until he heard her door slam, then whistling merrily, he went to get the pie Myrtle had left him for lunch.

Preparations and an Invitation

Myrtle, unaware of the war between Alfred and Nelly, was having a nice time at the patchwork club. It had been awkward at first, but once Mrs Grundy had looked her over and given a nod, the ladies became welcoming.

"Was there a particular quilt you wanted to make?" they asked.

"I want something cheerful, suitable for the grandchildren," Myrtle said, turning the pages of a quilting magazine thoughtfully.

"Do they live near," asked a nervous woman called Millicent Mable.

"No, but now that we live in the

country, I'm hoping they will stay with us. Their parents work and a nanny looks after them during the holidays. One of the reasons we bought the house is because it has a wonderful garden for the children to play in."

"That's nice, what age are they."

"Sally's seven and Peter's six."

"If you want camp-beds, Molly has a sale on them at the moment," said Mrs Moody.

Myrtle's hand flew to her mouth and she shook her head.

"Oh no, Alfred's building the beds. We want everything in the room to be special, that is why I want to make the quilts," she bit her lip uncertainly. "What colours should I make them?"

"Pink for the girl," said Mrs Grundy. Her nose and eyebrows were lifted and her closed eyelids fluttered most peculiarly.

The ladies of the club glanced at her nervously.

"Sally doesn't like p…" Myrtle started to say.

Edna Golding nudged her sharply with her elbow. "Pink is a marvellous colour for little girls," she said loudly.

All the ladies nodded their heads and babbled loudly about pink being the only colour.

"I think red and green would be cheerful," whispered Millicent Mable behind her hand.

Myrtle thought of the red shell-bucket and nodded. Mrs Grundy had not finished giving directions. Her voice cut across the babbling loudly. "And you will make a blue one for the boy, but not dark blue, I detest dark blue."

Navy blue was Peter's favourite colour, but Myrtle didn't say so. Instead, she changed the subject. "I'm hoping the children will come for Christmas. I'm getting the attic rooms ready for them."

33

The Britwhistles Win a Prize

Mrs Grundy nodded, and her eyes opened slowly as her nose lowered little by little. At this, the tension in the room relaxed. "Yes, an attic will work, you don't want children under your feet, but don't let them jump around, I can't abide the noise of children bouncing overhead."

Everyone nodded and murmured about the shocking noise of children.

Mrs Grundy stood up and shook the wrinkles out of her skirt. Seeing this, the others hastily got to their feet.

"Now that is settled, we will have lunch. I hope you sliced your sandwiches into triangles this time, Edna."

Edna nodded. "I've done them exactly the way you expect."

As the ladies moved towards the table, Mrs Jennings caught Myrtle's elbow and pulled her away from the crowd.

"You can choose whatever colours you like but say nothing about them." She winked. "If you don't draw attention to your quilts SHE will never notice."

Myrtle winked back, and so began her friendship with the ladies of the Patched-Up club.

As soon as she got home, Myrtle took the wooden cover off her sewing machine. It was an ancient machine and ran by turning a handle. It was black and went clickety-clack, clickety-clack, as she wound the handle round and round. Day after day the sound filled Toot Cottage as Myrtle stitched hundreds of little squares together.

As the months rolled by, Myrtle's quilts grew and Alfred's beds took shape, until one day Myrtle said:

"I think it's time to send the Christmas-Invitation."

"Don't you think October is a little early," said Alfred.

"If we leave it too late, Jillian and Bob will have made their Christmas plans and engaged a nanny for the holidays."

"We don't want that," said Alfred. "Let's send it soon."

So that afternoon the Britwhistles sent off a special letter and waited for the return post with excitement. But as the weeks passed and they heard nothing, excitement gave way to anxiety.

"Are you sure they got the invitation to come for Christmas?" said Alfred.

"Maybe they didn't, maybe the letter went astray," said Myrtle, her face brightening into a smile as hope arose.

"That must be it," said Alfred. "Perhaps we

should send a card, it's harder to lose."

Myrtle nodded and opened the lid of her scrapbooking box. "That's a splendid idea. I've got some pretty magazine pictures and seaside postcards we can cut up."

"No, not a homemade card, Myrtle, Molly has some clown ones with, 'I Wish You Were Here,' written inside them. Let's send one of those."

"A clown card, yes, that's ideal," said Myrtle, shutting the box.

They went to town that afternoon and argued a bit over which clown to choose because there was more than one, but at last, they found the right card. Then Myrtle (using her fancy ink pen) rewrote the invitation.

"Here, put these in too," said Alfred, popping two packets of stickers into the envelope.

Myrtle nodded approvingly, "fish for Peter and shells for Sally, I like that," then she licked the flap of the envelope and pressed it firmly shut. "I will pay extra and send it registered post. That way we will know for sure it gets there."

"Good idea, Myrtle, it will be well worth the money."

But the Christmas tree was up and there was still no letter. A reply came on Christmas Eve in the form of a large card full of sentimental verse and a stiff little handwritten sentence of regret. Myrtle put it on the mantlepiece next to the card Marmaduke (with Alfred's help) sent them each year.

"I really thought we might see the children this Christmas," said Myrtle, placing a parcel under the tree.

Alfred scrawled 'Myrtle' across a box and sat it beside the parcel.

"So did I."

"Can I put the quilts on the beds now?"

"There's no point bothering with sheets, Myrtle."

"I know, but at least I can see how my quilts look."

"In a minute, I just have to finish tightening the screws."

Alfred popped a screwdriver into his pocket, climbed the stairs and went into Peter's room. Myrtle's knees creaked as she slowly followed him up the steps. In her arms, she carried two quilts; a blue and yellow one for Peter and a red and green one for Sally. Alfred had nearly finished fixing Peter's bed when she stumped in, wheezing.

"You've made a superb job of these, Alfie," she said, stroking one of the big wooden knobs that stood at each corner of the bed.

Alfred finished screwing the bed-base down and dropped a mattress on top of it.

The Britwhistles Win a Prize

"Thanks."

He picked up his screwdriver again and wandered into Sally's room.

Myrtle spread Peter's quilt over the mattress and tweaked the corners into place before following him. "I just wish the children were here to see them."

"It's for the best," said Alfred, in a gruff voice. He shook the bed and screwed the legs on a little tighter. "There's lots more we need to do before these rooms are perfect. No bedroom is finished without a rocking chair."

Myrtle's face brightened as she spread Sally's quilt over the bed. "You are so right, of course there must be rocking chairs, and one quilt each is not enough, we might have a cold snap. I will make more quilts."

The Britwhistles first Christmas in Toot Cottage was quiet. Alfred was pleased with his new socks, and Myrtle loved her china teapot. She had made a tiny Christmas cake and bought a small roll of ham, which they ate with new potatoes and salad from the garden, and because it was a sweltering day, they finished with ice cream.

"Today is the beginning of a new year," said Alfred on New Year's Day, as he threw the Christmas tree on the compost pile. "I shall pick out the timber for the rocking chairs."

"Yes, a fresh start, anything can happen," said Myrtle. "I shall begin the quilts."

They ate the last of the leftover ham, and later that afternoon Alfred chopped down a maple tree while Myrtle cut oodles of brightly coloured squares. And all year, as Alfred turned chair-spindles and Myrtle stitched patches together, they thought of the merry time they would have when Sally and Peter came. By December, a rocking chair sat in each room while at the end of each bed lay an extra quilt. But on Christmas Eve a large card with a small regret sat next to the cat's card on the mantlepiece.

"I thought the children would come this year," said Myrtle. Her mouth drooped as she put a parcel under the Christmas tree.

The Britwhistles Win a Prize

"So did I," said Alfred putting a box beside it, "but it is for the best. The rooms are not ready yet."

Myrtle's eyes widened and her mouth fell open. "Aren't they?"

"No, there is nothing for them to store their clothes in when they come. I need to make two sets of drawers."

Myrtle beamed at him.

"You are such a clever man, of course the rooms are not ready. I need to make rugs for the floor and pictures for the walls."

That year Alfred chopped down an oak tree and made two sets of drawers while Myrtle braided rugs and worked Sally and Peter's names into cross-stitches. And the year after, Alfred made blanket boxes while Myrtle made curtains and more quilts.

And so, the years ticked by in a comfortable rhythm of housework, gardening, and outings. Easter, birthdays, and Christmases came and went. And in between all the activities and Alfred's pranks on Nelly, the Britwhistles worked at making everything perfect for Sally and Peter, until the two little rooms in the attic were bursting with quilts and furniture, a shell bucket, and a small fishing rod.

An Ill Wind

The big white cockatoos were settling in the gum trees as the light dimmed.

"Time for bed," said Alfred.

"So it is," said Myrtle. She shut the cat in the bathroom and lit a candle. Then they got into their pyjamas and climbed into an old-fashioned iron bed with a brass knob in each of the four corners. All the while, the roses on the wallpaper danced in time to the candle's flickering flame. Soon the cuckoo clock started chiming.

"When are you going to fix that clock, dearie? I love the sound of cuckoo clocks, but two hundred and fifty chimes are too much."

"One day," said Alfred, picking up his scruffy black Bible. He opened it at the page with the folded

41

corner.

"Oh Alfie, you say that every night," chuckled Myrtle. She picked up her Bible.

It got very quiet as they read. The only sounds were the wind in the trees and the cuckoo's repetitive little "who-who." Eventually, Myrtle put her Bible on the bedside table.

"Are you finished, Alfie?" she asked, leaning towards the candle.

"Yes, Myrtle-Turtle," said Alfred, putting his Bible down.

"Humph," blew Myrtle toward the flickering flame. The room went instantly black. They both lay quietly in the dark for a while, listening for who-who two-hundred-and-fifty. When the wee bird's door finally slammed shut, Alfred, as usual, was the first to speak.

"Listen to that, Myrtle," (he said it every night.)

"What dear?" (She knew the answer, but it would spoil the game to say anything else.)

"The silence..............no electronic buzzing."

"Isn't it peaceful," said Myrtle, acting surprised at his answer. And they lay there in the dark, happily talking over the highlights of the day as they did every night. Tonight, it was a poisonous spider in the woodshed for Alfred. For Myrtle, it was the bath plug turning up.

Wendy Hamilton

"When are you going to fix that clock?"

The Britwhistles Win a Prize

"Just when I had despaired of ever finding it," she said, "in the bottom of the ironing basket of all places."

The conversation pottered along pleasantly, like a slow train passing through expected stations, until the cricket that lived under the bedroom window started singing. Then Alfred whisked out of bed.

"Must you?" said Myrtle with a resigned sigh, "couldn't you leave the cricket alone tonight."

Alfred fell over his slippers and landed on the floor with a bang.

"It's annoying."

"It's a nice little noise," said Myrtle, lighting the candle again. She did not ask if he was hurt because he fell over his slippers every night.

"It is not."

Myrtle shook her head slowly. "I don't know why you bother; you never get it."

Alfred grabbed the fly-spray off his bedside table. "I will tonight."

He pulled up the window, leaned out, and blasted the sill with fly spray for a long time. When he finally slammed the window shut, the cricket was still singing, but the can was empty.

"I don't understand dearie, why a man who insists on growing things organically is so heavy-handed with fly-spray?"

"You will know when you are older," said Alfred, climbing back into bed. He used to say that to his children when they asked a question he couldn't answer.

Myrtle blew out the candle so he couldn't see her smiling. "Goodnight, Alfie."

"Goodnight, Myrtle-Turtle." Alfred closed his eyes and dropped instantly off to sleep.

But Myrtle, listening to Alfred slumbering beside her, had time to design a new quilt before she drifted into dreamland.

Every morning Alfred got up early to light the fire and feed the cat. "I'd like to get a gun and shoot those noisy birds," he said, as Myrtle came into the warm kitchen.

"Oh Alf, you are just a big softy under all that silly talk. Don't let Nelly hear you, she can't tell when you are joking and when you are serious. We could get into big trouble if anyone believed you really would shoot them."

Alfred opened the back door wide. "I would shoot them all if I had the chance,"

Myrtle put a pot on the stove and started stirring the porridge. While her back was turned, Alfred rolled a plum out the door to a cheeky cockatoo waiting expectantly at the bottom of the steps. The bird winked its beady eye at Alfred as it caught the plum with its foot.

"Oh Alf, you would not shoot them," said Myrtle, continuing to stir.

"Yes, I would," said Alfred, fishing in his pocket for dried apricots.

Myrtle shivered as she stirred. "There is a draft coming in. Don't open the door every morning while I'm making the porridge."

"Right oh Myrtle-Turtle," said Alfred cheerfully. He chucked a big handful of apricots to the waiting birds before shutting the door. Then he swaggered over to the table, pulled out a chair and sat down.

Myrtle put a bowl of porridge before Alfred and sat opposite him. Then they bowed their heads and shut their eyes.

"Thank you for this food dear Lord, Amen," prayed Alfred.

"Amen," said Myrtle. She opened her eyes, lifted a fat teapot and poured two cups of tea. "What are you doing this morning, Dear?" she said, setting the teapot down on the breadboard.

Alfred dug his spoon into his porridge.

"I thought I might weed the runner beans."

Myrtle smiled and nodded.

"They could do with weeding."

"What are your plans, Myrtle?" asked Alfred,

picking up a cup and taking a slurp.

Myrtle tapped her spoon on her false teeth and gazed out the window. "I'm not sure which way the wind is blowing this morning. I shall have to see how I feel after I've washed the dishes. I dare say I will know by then."

"I dare say you will."

They chatted about the beans and the blight on the peach tree as they ate. Once breakfast was over, Myrtle cleared the table and Alfred went out to the garden. When Alfred came inside a little later, he saw a polishing-wind was blowing about. He knew it was a polishing-wind because Myrtle was rummaging through the bottom of the hutch dresser and that was where she kept the furniture polish and soft rags.

"While you are in there, pass me the string," said Alfred, tiptoeing in his boots across the clean floor.

With her head still in the cupboard, Myrtle pulled out a ball of string and waved it in his direction.

"Thanks," said Alfred, tiptoeing out again.

The door banged shut as Myrtle found the round tin with the smiling bee on the lid. Furniture polishing when you are in the right mood is a pleasant job. Myrtle put a dollop of polish on a thick yellow cloth and rubbed away at the oak sideboard until it glowed. The smell of honey-wax filled the room and she hummed cheerfully. It was a small house and Myrtle had lots of energy. It did not take long to polish everything downstairs. She gave the last vigorous wipe to the kitchen table and gazed at the staircase. As she gazed, she stopped humming, her shoulders slumped and energy drained from her body. She avoided going upstairs these days. She breathed in deeply as she shifted her eyes to the kitchen ceiling.

"It must be done, the dust is gathering," she said to the light bulb. With that, she mounted the stairs slowly.

Alfred found her sitting in Sally's rocking chair sometime later, still clutching her polishing cloth.

"Good grief, is it morning tea time already?" exclaimed Myrtle, getting up as quickly as her knees would let her.

"It is indeed." Alfred peered at his wife. "Now then, Honey, what's troubling you?"

"Only the usual," said Myrtle, dabbing her eyes with the corner of the polishing rag. "And I confess I have allowed myself more than five minutes of self-pity," she added, going red in the face.

Alfred patted her hand.

"Never mind Love, come and have a cup of tea."

And together they slowly descended the stairs. Alfred put the kettle on the stove without his

48

normal bustle and Myrtle cut the cake quietly. It did not escape Alfred's notice that his slice of cake was larger than usual, or that his wife said nothing about watching their waistlines. No polishing wind was blowing about now; instead, an ill wind was blowing. The day that started so briskly was dwindling into gloominess. Suddenly Alfred had an idea.

"What say we go fishing Myrtle? The day is still young and I feel in my bones the fish are biting."

"I say, what a marvellous idea Alfred," said Myrtle perking up immediately. "We haven't been for a ride in Lulu for ages. It's a lovely day, just perfect for the beach. See if there are any tomatoes and cucumbers in the garden while I get the picnic basket."

"Just the ticket," said Alfred. He grabbed a bowl off the bench and rushed out.

Meanwhile, Myrtle opened the door under the stairs. It was dark in the cupboard and smelled faintly of mouse. Normally the smell of mouse worried Myrtle, but today she did not think about it; her head was too full of waves and sand. Instead of baiting traps with cheese, she peered through the gloom until she spotted a square wicker basket peeping out from behind an oil heater. Unfortunately, that was not all, a set of wooden steps were also in the way and a long fluorescent light tube. Alfred picking ripe tomatoes heard thumps and bangs and a loud SMASH. He rushed down the garden path and burst through the back door.

"Are you alright Myrtle?" he shouted anxiously.

"Oh yes," replied Myrtle placidly.

The picnic basket sat calmly on the table and the cupboard was closed once again. Of the kitchen steps, there was no sign. "I'll make lunch while you get the fishing stuff," she said, sweeping fragments of the fluorescent tube into a dustpan.

"Right oh," said Alfred reassured. He bustled out to his workshop to look for his tackle box and rod.

Then Myrtle heard thumps and bangs. But as thumps and bangs were always coming from the back shed, she took no notice at all.

After a loud smash, Alfred poked his head into the kitchen sheepishly. "I hope you didn't want that lampshade," he said, shuffling his feet awkwardly.

"Which one?"

"The yellow and red lead-light one."

"Oh, that one, I've been waiting so long for you to fix the broken bit, I forgot I owned it," said Myrtle kindly.

"Oh good," said Alfred, bouncing in. "Are you ready yet?"

"Almost," said Myrtle. "I just need to change into my sailor suit and find my hat."

Alfred slapped his forehead. "That reminds me, I need my fishing hat," he said whisking away.

Nelly (hidden in the bushes) watched all the activity.

"They must have gone fishing for the day," she said to Molly later that morning. "I saw them load up the truck."

"They might not have gone fishing," said Molly.

"Oh yes, they have. He was carrying a fishing rod and she was wearing that ridiculous outfit she always wears when she goes to the beach."

"Which outfit?"

"The blue dress with the wide white collar and the straw hat with the long ribbons."

"Her sailor suit, you're right Nelly, they will have gone to the beach."

Nelly sniffed. "Why does she wear such strange clothes? Why doesn't she wear jeans and tee-shirts like normal people?"

"She is her own person," said Molly, who by now knew the Britwhistles well.

"Quite frankly," said Nelly haughtily, "I think she looks like Mary Poppins grown old.

Molly looked at Nelly's worn jeans and sweatshirt and raised one eyebrow. She thought Myrtle looked a lot smarter than Nelly did. "Oh, leave her alone," she said abruptly. "I think she looks very nice. We don't all think alike, and that is good."

"Humph," said Nelly.

"Is it possible for that woman to leave this shop without flouncing off in a huff?" Molly asked her husband, as Nelly slammed the door. "You had better tighten the doorbell, Wilbur," she added, glancing at the brass bell hanging above the door. "It gets such a walloping every time she comes and goes."

"She certainly is forceful," he agreed, pulling a stepladder out from under the counter. He dragged it over to the door and was about to climb on it when something out the window caught his eye. "I say," he said in alarm, "the Britwhistle's have had an accident! The front of their truck is all smacked up!"

The Fishing Trip

The fishing trip started well enough. Alfred whistled as he backed Lulu out of the workshop and drove her slowly to the back door. The Britwhistles loved Lulu. She was a red truck with a tiny house behind her cab.

Myrtle swung the passenger door open and hoisted herself onto the seat.

"I'm glad we're doing this," she said, slamming the door shut and peering into the rear vision mirror. "Are you sure the hamper won't fall over, Alfie?"

"Quite sure, I wedged it under the table. Now Myrtle, where do you want to go?"

"What about Church Beach?" she answered, scrubbing furniture polish off her cheek with a hanky.

The Britwhistles Win a Prize

"Good idea," said Alfred

He eased Lulu down the driveway and out to the road. Once they got through town, he sped up. Myrtle hummed as they buzzed along the country road that wound through low hills covered with golden grass. Church Beach was not far away and not its actual name. Its real name, however, was so long and had so many moos and loos, bongs, and gongs in it, the Britwhistles named it after a quaint little church near the bay. Before long, the church loomed in front of them.

"My goodness!" Myrtle exclaimed, staring over the rim of her glasses, "look at all those people."

"It must be a working bee," said Alfred, as they moved towards it rapidly. "I suppose they are restoring the church for the hundred-year centennial next month."

Myrtle twisted her head and read the sign in the front yard as they whizzed past.

"Yes, that's it."

"Don't forget to look at the blackberry patch as we go by."

Myrtle turned her head to the other side of the road. "Of course not,"

"Can you see any?"

"Yes."

"Are there any black ones or are they still red?"

Myrtle craned her neck further and further back as they moved forward. "There are a few red ones, but there are lots of black ones,"

Alfred's face split into a wide smile. "Goody, we will stop there on the way home."

The wheels kept spinning and before long they reached their destination. Church Beach was a pretty bay with a long wharf. It was lunchtime when they arrived, so they had lunch sitting at the tiny table in the house on the back of the truck. Once the picnic basket was empty and the teacups washed and put away, Alfred made straight for the end of the wharf. He did not walk like an old man; he swung his tackle box and bucket as he strode along, whistling. By the time Myrtle caught up, he had baited his hook and thrown out his line several times.

"Look at those big ones down there, Myrtle," he said, leaning so far over the side of the wharf he nearly fell in. "I wish I had a net and a stick of dynamite!"

"It has only been five minutes," said Myrtle, putting down her bag. She opened the folding chair she was carrying. "You have to be patient."

"I've got plenty of patience," said Alfred, impatiently jiggling his line. He hoped the movement might snag a fish by the gills. "They are not biting today. I'm sick of fishing, let's go and get an ice-cream from the general store."

"We have only just got here, Dear, at least try for another ten minutes. See if you can get that big one for dinner." She took a book out of her bag and settled into her chair. Chapter one, School Holidays, she read.

"Look at that biggie," said Alfred loudly.

"Shhh, Dear, the fish will hear you." She vaguely thought silence had something to do with catching fish. She looked down at her book again.

"Missed him! Hold my rod, Myrtle, while I untangle the line."

Myrtle reached out and grabbed it without looking up. Alfred twiddled with the line for a few minutes before pulling it out of her hand.

"I'll have it now."

Myrtle nodded and turned a page. Meanwhile, Alfred threw the line back in the water and sat on the upturned fish-bucket. He sat there quietly, long enough for Myrtle to read three more pages. On the fourth page, he wound in his line.

"It's no good, the fish are not biting."

Myrtle shut her book with a sigh and put it in her bag; she knew what was coming next.

"I think we should get an ice-cream now."

Myrtle struggled out of her seat and folded it up. "It's far too early for an ice-cream. We always get them on the way home."

"Couldn't we have two today?"

Myrtle looked meaningfully at his wide girth. "It's a lovely day, Dear, why don't you take some pictures with your birthday-camera."

"That's a good idea," said Alfred, brightening. He rushed down the wharf and into Lulu.

That was the best present I ever bought him, thought Myrtle, following slowly. When she reached the sand, she opened her chair again and set it down under a tree.

"Where is it?" yelled Alfred from the open door of the house truck.

"It's in there somewhere, Love, try the cupboard." Myrtle sat down and opened her book.

"I found it," said Alfred, shutting the door, "it was in a big pot."

"See if you can get some nice pictures of the rocks over there," said Myrtle.

Alfred squinted at them. "Good idea," he said.

He stumped off and shrank into a dot in the distance. For a whole hour, Myrtle read without interruption as her husband shot rocks and seagulls with his camera. The rest of the afternoon was also quiet, because he was searching for the lens cap. The shade of the tree had shifted off Myrtle by the time he came stomping up the beach towards her.

The Britwhistles Win a Prize

He looked like a boiled lobster, but it was difficult to say if it was sunburn or triumph over finding his camera lens.

"Let's go, Myrtle."

Myrtle put her book in her bag and picked up the empty fish bucket. "What about a cup of tea before we go? Be a love and make it while I collect a few shells."

"Alright, and then we will go to the general store."

Myrtle did not want lots of shells and the gas stove in Lulu heated the water swiftly, so it was not long before Alfred parked the truck outside the general store. The general store was a wonderful shop. It was a seaside version of Molly's Emporium; it sold buckets and spades, groceries, car oil, surfboards, and anything else you might want at the beach.

"Bizzz," went the door buzzer loudly as the Britwhistle's entered. Their feet made clunking noises as they clumped over the wide floorboards. A fat woman shuffled from the backroom to the counter through a beaded curtain.

"Mmm smell that," said Alfred sniffing deeply. "General-store is the best smell in the world. Do they make air fresheners that smell of general stores?"

Myrtle was about to say "what a silly question,"

when she remembered samples of New-Car and Fresh-Washing. "I don't think so," she said uncertainly.

Alfred sniffed the air like a dog. "Perhaps I should invent one. It's a mixture of strawberries and washing powder, crayons and apples, with strong undertones of new gumboots." He walked over to the refrigerator. "Just listen to this fridge. This is the noisiest fridge in the world," he said happily. "Now then Myrtle, what will you have?" he asked, taking his wallet out of his back pocket. He hoped she might try something more adventurous than usual.

"Vanilla dipped in chocolate," said Myrtle, disappointingly. "What will you have today?"

"I can't decide," said Alfred Henry, looking at his wife slyly. "Which do you think I should have, the Marmite Chocolate Bomb or the Traffic Light?"

"Ooh, marmite and chocolate sound disgusting together." Myrtle shuddered, as he hoped she would. "Have a nice vanilla one. Your tongue always looks hideous after you have had one of those Traffic Lights."

"I'll have a Traffic Light," said Alfred Henry, promptly picking one out of the freezer and putting it on the counter.

"Don't do such long licks, Love," said Myrtle, as they walked along the beach eating their ice creams. "It looks yucky."

The naughty boy in Alfred was hoping she would say something like that. He turned to face her, opened his mouth wide and stuck out his tongue.

"Ooh shut your mouth old man, I don't want to see your tongue, it looks horrible," squealed Myrtle much to his delight.

He skipped around his wife, poking his tongue in and out while she pretended to hit him. Then Alfred patted damp sand into a ball and threw it at Myrtle, and Myrtle (putting the last of her ice cream in her mouth) picked up a long string of seaweed and biffed it at Alfred. And they danced about the sand like two big kids throwing sand balls at one another's legs. And whenever Myrtle showed signs of giving up on the fight, Alfred kept it going by poking his tongue at her. In this way, the sand-balls kept flying and everything went along very merrily until Myrtle squealed:

"Ooh put your tongue away, nobody wants to see a green and yellow tongue."

"Ha, ha, yes they would. Peter would love a good traffic-light-tongue," shouted Alfred jubilantly. He said it without thinking.

Myrtle instantly stopped dancing, and broke her ice-cream stick in half as she gazed across the sea with a faraway look in her eyes.

"So he would," she said quietly.

Alfred also lost all his playfulness.

"So he would," he echoed. His head drooped and he dragged a small curve in the sand with his foot. "I'm sorry Myrtle, I wasn't thinking, I shouldn't have said that."

Myrtle did not seem to hear him. "It's a pity Sally is not here," she said, "Sally would have liked collecting shells."

"Yes, she would have."

A seat was nearby; they walked to it and sat down. Myrtle took off her watch and put it on her knee where they could both see it. They sat there very quietly and sadly, watching the minute hand. When five minutes were up, Myrtle shook herself and strapped her watch back on her wrist. "It can't be helped that our grandchildren live so far away," she said with brittle cheerfulness.

"That's right, Myrtle," said Alfred bravely. "They will come one day and then Peter and I will eat six Traffic-Lights all at once."

"And Sally and I will collect so many shells we'll have trouble getting them all in Lulu."

Alfred squeezed her hand and nodded. "Yes, you will, and then they will play in the garden."

Myrtle smiled at him and squeezed his hand back. "And they will sleep in the lovely beds you built, Alfie, under the quilts I made for them."

"Let's stop at the blackberry patch by the church on the way home," said Alfred, having a happy thought at just the right time. "Didn't you say you saw some?"

"Yes lets," agreed Myrtle perking up. "I saw plump ones on the bushes. If we get enough, I will make us a blackberry pie for dinner."

They climbed into the truck and Alfred put it into gear. But the gear stick that usually moved smoothly, made a horrible grinding noise.

"Sorry Lulu," said Alfred, flustered. They returned home by the same road they came, but the golden hills of the morning had disappeared; in their place was brown parched land. They rounded a corner and the church loomed into sight. Alfred Britwhistle had driven past the church without mishap many times, but this time was different; Lulu, instead of sticking to the road as she always did, suddenly veered off and hit the side of the church.

"Watch out!" screamed Myrtle, ducking and throwing her arm in front of her face.

There was a big bang as the truck came to a sickening halt.

"Oh Alfred," said Myrtle, as people ran towards them. "This day is going from worse to worse."

"It certainly is," said Alfred, opening his door with difficulty.

Everyone was very nice about the hole Lulu made in the wall. They pretended it was small and easily fixed; which was especially nice, as they had just finished painting it.

"Don't worry about it," said the vicar.

"Anyone could mistake the accelerator for the brake," said the church organist.

"Watch out the school down the road doesn't jump out in front of you Granddad," teased the hooligan on probation. Everyone frowned at him. The court sent him to help paint, and he had been trying the deacon's patience all morning.

But for once Alfred did not feel like joking or teasing.

"Don't let this knock your confidence," said the deacon, scowling at the hooligan.

It was good advice. Nevertheless, Alfred's confidence was shaken.

"I think it is time to hang up the car keys," he said to Myrtle as they rode home in the tow-truck. "Drop Lulu round the back," he said to the truck driver as he took his wallet from his pocket.

That night Myrtle did not blow out the candle as quickly as usual.

The Britwhistles Win a Prize

The Britwhistle's have an accident.

Instead, they lay in bed looking at the flickering shadows on the wall. It was very quiet in the room. The only sound was the clock ticking. The cricket had nothing to fear from the spray can this evening; he sang as usual, but his enemy did not seem to hear. At length, Alfred spoke. Not his usual comment about silence and lack of electricity. What he said was something quite different.

"What if I had hit a child?" he said with a shudder. "What if it was Peter or Sally?"

"You are right," said Myrtle, "they can't fix a child like a hole in the wall."

"I will never drive our grandchildren to the

beach," said Alfred mournfully.

"I will never collect shells with Sally," said Myrtle softly.

"Peter and I will never do traffic light tongues." Alfred's face was sad as he wound up the clock and set the alarm. "I'm giving us an extra ten minutes," he said. "I think we need it."

Myrtle said nothing. She just patted his hand in agreement. So, they lay there, side by side, feeling their loss. After fifteen minutes, the alarm rang.

"There's a train that goes past the beach and it is an easy walk to the station," said Myrtle, brightening up.

"Yes, there is," said Alfred, smiling. "It's only two-dollars-fifty on Saturdays and children are half price."

"We don't need a truck to enjoy our grandchildren," said Myrtle.

"That's right," said Alfred in a firm voice. "Besides, Molly sells Traffic Light ice creams."

"Of course she does, Alfie," said Myrtle loudly. "A hideous tongue in the park is just as good as a hideous tongue at the beach." She leaned over and blew out the candle with a strong huff.

"We can walk most places," said Alfred.

"Yes, we can, Alfie. Perhaps Sally and Peter might like Lulu as a playhouse?"

The Britwhistles Win a Prize

"I'm sure they would, Myrtle. She would make a super-duper playhouse."

"Goodnight."

"Goodnight."

Alfred dropped off to sleep like a pebble falling off a cliff. But Myrtle lay awake for a long time, planning quilts and curtains for Sally and Peter's new playhouse.

Soap Making and a Surprise

The windmill on Alfred's workshop went around and around like a wheel on a bicycle. Myrtle sat at the kitchen table listening to its tinny squeak as she eyed a fishbowl on a tea trolley in the bathroom.

"Is the windmill generating enough wind to run the food processor, Alfred?" said Myrtle.

"More power than you need, even the iron and toaster will work with that wind."

"Good. I shall make soap this morning. There's only one bar left."

Alfred nodded. "I noticed the fishbowl was getting low." He stroked the bald part of his head, "We don't want to run out. I want to keep my thick hair in good condition."

67

The Britwhistles Win a Prize

Soap Making Day.

"My dear, we are not going through that again! You say these foolish things to Nelly without thinking. Then the next thing I know, we have the health inspector at our door. Fortunately, he was a reasonable man. Another inspector may actually believe my soap dissolved your hair."

"No harm done," said Alfred, dismissing the incident with a wave of his hand.

"No harm done? Cecily Hampton has a shampoo allergy and our soap could help her, but because of your tall tales I can't give her any."

"Oh dear," said Alfred, looking guilty. "Just show the little girl your hair and tell her you wash it with soap every night."

"I tried that Alfred and I explained it is only caustic for the first three weeks, but she won't believe me."

Alfred's eyes sparkled. "Perhaps I could tell her it was a joke and explain how the chemicals form."

"And that is another thing, Alfred. I don't want you using the fridge as a whiteboard. The markers don't rub off easily."

"You're no fun," said Alfred sulkily.

"Save science lessons for Thursday Alfie, the blokes at your club will be interested."

"Alright," said Alfred, cheering up.

Because it was soap-making-day, Myrtle skipped

sweeping the floor.

"Do you want any help, Myrtle?"

"No, I am better doing this by myself," she said, pulling on rubber gloves, "you can go out into the garden if you like."

"Good oh, what time will lunch be today; when the dog-walking man comes past?"

Myrtle glanced at the clock before bending down and pulling cake tins from the cupboard. "I doubt I'll be finished by then." She straightened up and put the tins on the bench. "Let's try for the truck, if not, it will be the jogging-lady."

"Alright," said Alfred, taking his hat off a peg by the back door.

"And Alfie," said Myrtle, putting a jar of oil and a bunch of lavender beside the cake tins, "have another look in the workshop for your watch. It's ridiculous how many you've lost. You must be able to find at least one of them if you look hard enough."

Alfred opened the door and was about to 'say alright' again, but the wind whipped the words from his mouth and blew the lavender to the floor. By the time he got the door shut and Myrtle picked up the lavender, neither of them remembered the lost watches.

Myrtle made a batch of soap, poured it into a big cake tin and sprinkled lavender over it. Then she made several more batches because the fishbowl was almost empty. When the soap was as hard as cheese, she cut it into rectangular bars. Although each step was quite quick, she was still cutting soap when the frozen food truck rumbled past the gate. It rattled the pictures on the wall and made the knife in Myrtle's hand slip.

"Blast that truck," said Myrtle, looking at the misshapen bars of soap. She felt tired and her back ached. Worst of all, her forehead felt itchy and she could not scratch it without going through the whole rigmarole of taking off her rubber gloves. She chose instead to put up with it, which of course made it seem ten times worse.

Suddenly the back door flew open and Alfred blew in with a great whoosh. His cheeks were rosy and his meagre hair was a thin rim of spikes.

"Is lunch ready? I heard the lunchtime truck go past."

"No, it is not!" said Myrtle crossly. "I haven't cleaned up yet. Lunch will not be until the jogging-lady, after all.

"Very good," said Alfred, ignoring his wife's crossness. He was about to go back into the garden when something unexpected happened. There was a rumble and a rattle, and all the pictures on the wall slid to the left. The Britwhistle's mouths dropped open and they looked at each other in astonishment.

"That was another frozen food truck!" said Myrtle, "can you believe it? That's two in one day!"

Alfred went to the front room and looked out the window, "and there are more coming," he said in astonishment.

"My goodness," said Myrtle, "in a bigger town I would think nothing of it, but in Woolamoloo?"

"It certainly is strange," said Alfred, "I wonder what is happening?"

If you wanted local gossip, you could not do better than Nelly.

"Let's have lunch on the veranda," said Myrtle. "It's messy in here."

"That is a cunning idea," said Alfred, guessing her real intention. "Nobody in their right mind would eat out there in all this wind. I expect our nosy neighbour will be over to see what we are up to."

"You have me all wrong," teased Myrtle with a mischievous twinkle in her eye, "I only meant we can have lunch quicker."

"Sure," chuckled Alfred disbelievingly. "I expect Nelly will have a sudden urge to bake this afternoon."

"Whatever gives you that idea Alfie?" smiled Myrtle. It did not take long to get lunch set out on the small table on the veranda. They had barely buttered their bread before Nelly, her hair blowing in all directions, skittered down the front path.

"I thought I would do some baking this afternoon but I've run out of sugar," she shouted, holding out an empty jar, "could I borrow some?"

"Certainly," hollered Myrtle above the wind as she took the jar. "Would you like to join us for a bite to eat or are you too busy?"

"I think I can make time," said Nelly, plunking herself into a rocking chair.

"Look at that, another truck" shouted Alfred, as a lorry rumbled past.

"Cake, Nelly?" asked Myrtle, pouring her a cup of tea.

"Yes please."

"The factory has quadrupled its output," said Nelly loudly.

Information from Nelly was always plentiful but dodgy. "It's like oysters," Alfred said behind her back. "You have to open a lot of shells before you find a pearl." Over the years Alfred had perfected the art of winding his neighbour up. He looked at her doubtfully. "Are you sure?" he said in a disbelieving tone as he handed her the cup of tea.

"They certainly have!" said Nelly, sticking her chin out. "You'll see. That's why there are so many trucks today."

Alfred and Myrtle looked at each other and nodded their heads. They were very tiny nods, so small Nelly completely missed them.

"Fancy!" said Myrtle. She put a slab of fruitcake onto a plate and passed it over the table.

"Such goings-on, there will be trucks roaring up and down here like a highway, night and day," said Nelly, leaning back in her chair and taking a huge bite of cake.

"You don't say?"

The Britwhistles looked at each other again. This time, however, they shook their heads just the teensiest little bit.

"They've taken on lots more workers. Some of them are foreigners."

Alfred nodded at Myrtle. "Is that right?"

Nelly shuddered. "We'll all be murdered in our beds." She said it gloomily, with great satisfaction.

"I hope not!" said Myrtle, turning her head and rolling her eyes at Alfred.

"There is a new housing estate in Wollondilly." Nelly drained her cup and put it down. It made a sharp click as it hit the saucer.

"More tea, Nelly?" asked Alfred.

"Yes thanks," said Nelly holding out her cup. "I just hope they stay on their side," she said, flicking her head backwards in the direction of the hill behind the Britwhistle's vegetable garden. "That lot are all thugs and gangsters."

"Surely not?" said Myrtle mildly, shaking her head. "Why are you out here having lunch in all this wind?" asked Nelly, pulling the collar of her coat up around her neck.

"Wind, what wind?" said Alfred Henry. He opened his blue eyes wide. It was the same look he used when Nelly accused him of fake vomit or rubber snakes.

"Humph," she snorted. She flew out of her chair and flounced down the pathway in a rage.

"It is like pulling a cat's tail when I give her that look," said Alfred Henry proudly.

"Oh Alfie, that was naughty," giggled Myrtle.

"It was rather. What a pity, she has forgotten her sugar," said Alfred insincerely. He picked up the sugar jar. "Do you think I should call her back and apologise, Myrtle?"

"Oh, I don't think that will be necessary this time," said Myrtle, pretending to frown. "I think she will decide she's not into baking after all."

"It's rather cold out here," said Alfred, getting serious again. He pulled his hat lower to cover his ears.

"So it is," said Myrtle, looking at their cheese

sandwiches. "Put these in the oven while I clear the soap stuff off the kitchen table. I think they would be nicer toasted."

"Right oh," said Alfred, picking up the plates of sandwiches.

"I think tomorrow we should go for a walk and see what's going on behind the hill," said Alfred later, as they munched melted cheese on toast. He slid a chunk of cheese down the side of the chair to the waiting cat. "Do you think you would be up to it, Myrtle?"

"I think so," said Myrtle. The cat stretched his front feet onto Alfred's knees and the movement caught her attention. "Are you feeding that cat again Alfie? You know the vet said he was getting too fat."

Alfred pushed the cat under the table, out of sight. "Do you think you're up to the walk, Myrtle?" he repeated. "We haven't been around the back of the hill for ages. Funny to think there are houses there now. I still think of it as Bill Gordon's bull paddock."

"I wonder if the cattle-yard is still there?" said Myrtle, forgetting the cat. "So long as you don't go too fast, I would be up to a long walk. If my knees find it a bit much, we can take the bus home. I must admit, I'm curious to see what's been happening."

The Other Side of the Hill

It was sunny when the Britwhistles set off for Wollondilly the next morning. They walked along the street... past Molly's Emporium...round the corner...through town...past the marble-soldier marooned on the traffic island...left at the library... and onto the water-clock. At the water-clock, they stopped. Myrtle sat on a park bench to rest her legs while Alfred examined the clock. The clock was huge and stood in a shallow pool. Alfred and several boys wandered about marvelling at the water that splashed through wheels and cogs, levers and knobs, pipes, pivots and buckets.

"Why's it only got one hand, Mr?" asked a small boy with tousled hair and grimy shorts.

The Britwhistles Win a Prize

Alfred put his hands on his hips, leaned back and stared up at the enormous face of the clock. "It's not meant to count minutes." He answered in a tone of authority because he had read the brass plaque mounted on the rim of the pool.

"It's no good at counting hours either," said a big boy. He was the proud owner of a watch and could tell the time.

Alfred loved the clock and was unwilling to admit its faults. He dug his hands deep into his pockets and rocked onto his toes. "That's because they measured time differently in the olden days," he bluffed.

"No, they didn't," said the watch-boy.

"Yes, they did," said Alfred, his eyebrows jutting out. He was beginning to dislike Watch-Boy. "What's your name sonny?"

"Butch," said Watch-Boy.

"Suits you," said Alfred, hoping to change the subject.

"How did they count it then?" said Butch in an aggressive tone.

"You will know when you are older," said Alfred, thinking Butch was a repulsive boy. He swung round on his heel. "I think it's time we moved on Myrtle," he called out, moving away from the water-clock.

"That was very quick," said Myrtle, looking up

from her book. (The clock was usually worth two chapters.)

"I don't think I want to stay here any longer," said Alfred, turning his head and scowling at the boys paddling in the pool. "I'm keen to get on if you have had enough rest."

"Oh yes," said Myrtle, closing her book and putting it in her bag. "I'm ready to go."

They walked on until they came to a small humped bridge which in the rainy season a river flowed under. There was no river today, however, just a deep ditch of cracked mud. Myrtle was glad because a bridge usually meant delay; even small creeks will float sticks and paper boats. As it was, Alfred insisted on hitting every pipe of the safety rail with the handle of his pocket knife; bong... bing... ping... pong....

They walked over the bridge and rounded a corner.

"My goodness, where have all these come from?" exclaimed Myrtle.

Alfred let out a long whistle of surprise. "Nelly wasn't making it up when she said a lot of people have shifted into the area," he said, staring at all the new houses.

"Mr Gordon must have sold his farm to a developer," said Myrtle. "There are no bulls now, that's for sure."

"Look at that big house where the cattle-yard used to be," said Alfred, his eyes growing rounder and rounder as they walked on.

"They have pulled down the cowshed," said Myrtle, turning her head to look at the other side of the road. "There must be children in the area. That's a big park."

"Swings and a flying-fox!" said Alfred, getting excited. He crossed the road swiftly.

"No, Alfred!" called out Myrtle, looking anxious. She crossed the road and caught up with him. "You are too big for the swings and too old for the flying-fox, and I don't want you sneaking back here with your skateboard to try out the track. Remember what happened with the roller skates. It was lucky you didn't break your hip!"

Alfred's face fell. He gave his wife the same look he gave Butch. They might have had a big argument there and then if they had not discovered the pond.

"Oh Alfred," said Myrtle, clapping her hands as she looked through the trees. "This is so much nicer than the old water hole."

"It certainly is," said Alfred, walking towards the pond, his temper suddenly quite restored. "They have dug it wider and deeper."

"Yes and landscaped it. It's very nicely planted out. Look at all the barbeques. We could bring Sally and Peter here to feed the ducks and picnic," said Myrtle without thinking.

Alfred picked up a long stick and poked about in the water. "We could," he said, "Peter and I could hunt for eels here." They both were so excited by their discovery neither of them felt the need to sit down for five minutes.

"Let's see if the factory looks different," said Alfred, tearing himself away from the pond at last.

"All right," said Myrtle.

They walked on, past row upon row of houses and side streets until they came to large gates made from grey metal pipes.

"These are new," said Alfred. "You used to be able to drive right in."

"They could have made them look a bit prettier," said Myrtle, wrinkling her nose.

"I suppose you would like curly wrought iron ones with pillars and stone lions," smiled Alfred.

"Of course," said Myrtle, knowing it was a silly wish, "just as I would rather have a castle than that ugly old factory."

"That factory may be ugly but it is not old," said Alfred peering through the closed gate. "Last time I was here it was less than half the size." '

The Britwhistles Win a Prize

A big truck roared out of the factory.

"It seems Nelly was more right than I thought. We won't be able to mark time with trucks soon. There will be too many of them."

"Mmm," said Myrtle thoughtfully. She was looking at the tall conifer trees that grew in a dense wall along the fence line. "Last time we were here those trees were only tiny."

While they stood there, the gates slowly swung open.

"They must be automatic," said Alfred, stepping back towards the edge of the road.

"They must be," agreed Myrtle, following him. "There is no sign of anyone. I suppose the switch is in the building."

While they were looking a big truck roared out of the factory and through the gates. As it passed them, the driver stuck his head out the window and yelled, "can't you read?"

"How rude!" said Myrtle, upset, "We weren't doing any harm!"

"I suppose he was referring to that notice," said Alfred, pointing to a large sign on the slowly closing gate.

"We hadn't gone in," said Myrtle, still upset. "They used to be much friendlier."

"You never needed to be an 'Authorized Personal' to visit when Archie was the manager," said Alfred, looking at the top part of the sign.

"Nobody minded us picking blackberries in there when we first shifted here," said Myrtle, looking at the 'Keep Out,' underneath.

"Times are changing," said Alfred.

"And not necessarily for the better," said Myrtle, still thinking about the rude truck driver. "Let's go home, I have seen all I want to see."

"Yes," said Alfred. "I'm glad there's a hill between us and progress."

The Bloomingdales

The man at the heart of the activity in the chicken factory was Mr Bloomingdale. Harry Bloomingdale was a salesman; a very good salesman. So good, the factory had to expand to keep up with all the frozen chickens he sold. He and his wife, Sandra, and their two children lived in the big house where the cattle-yard used to be. It was a grey brick house and lay in the path of the shadow of an enormous tree on the hill behind it. At the back of the house was a covered outdoor area where the potted ferns and barbeque lived. At the front was a door with seven windows and a patio on which stood a row of pots. The pots were Sandra's vegetable garden. Compared to the Britwhistles large sprawling garden Sandra's garden was barely a garden at all, nevertheless, she tended it with a great deal of care. At that moment she was inside leafing through a gardening book.

"What is wrong with my tomatoes?" she muttered, "they should look like these."

"Daddy will fix them when he comes home," said Billy, leaning against the couch his mother sat on.

"They will be eaten by then, Love," said Sandra, reaching out and smoothing his hair.

"Why is Daddy always away?"

"He has to travel a lot with his job, Sweetheart."

Billy sighed and kicked his legs. "Will he get home before I start school?"

Sandra laughed, "I should hope so, he'll be home long before two years are up."

She squinted at the book once more. "I wonder if these are the same brand of tomatoes as mine," she murmured.

"What was that you said, Mum?" said Billy, swinging on the arm of the couch.

"Be a love and bring me the packet of seeds I left on the hall table," said Sandra in a preoccupied tone of voice.

Billy let go of the couch and meandered over to the table in the front entrance.

Wendy Hamilton

There was a knock on the front door .

The Britwhistles Win a Prize

He was about to pick up the packet of seeds when there was a knock on the door. "Mummy, someone's here," he shouted in excitement. He peered through a lower window to see who it was, but all he could see was an enormous stomach bulging out over a belt buckle.

Sandra put her book aside and stood up. As she walked towards the door, her daughter darted out of her bedroom and rushed past her.

"Be careful, Mandy, you nearly knocked me over."

"Sorry Mum," said Mandy, "it might be Jane, she said she might come over this afternoon once she's done her homework."

"It's not Jane," said Billy, "it's Mr Gordon or Mr Grantham. Why do they have twin stomachs even though they're not brothers?"

"Hush, Billy, he might hear you," said Sandra, opening the door.

"Hello Mrs. Bloomingdale," said Mr Gordon. "I wondered if you would like these? It's been a bumper season and the wife and I can't eat them all." He held out a bag of tomatoes.

"Thank you, Mr Gordon, we would love them." Sandra put the bag on the hall table. "Mine aren't doing so well. Would you mind giving me a few tips?"

Mr Gordon liked people asking his opinion on gardening. He puffed out his chest and sucked in his stomach. "I'd be glad to, what's the problem?"

Sandra led the way to the first tomato plant. "They look a bit pale, perhaps it is because they are in pots? I always feel plants are better in the ground than pots, but the big tree out the back shades everything so I thought I would try them out here. The front is sunnier and better sheltered from the wind."

"They should be alright if you keep them well-watered, maybe a bit of liquid fertiliser would help," said Mr Gordon, inspecting Sandra's pot garden. "Your Tuscan cabbages look alright."

Mandy's mother looked over at the crinkly green plants and smiled. "Yes, I'm pleased with them, but I've noticed a few holes in the leaves."

"Probably slugs," said Mr Gordon.

"I know." Sandra sighed. "I don't like to put poison down because of the children."

"Use salt."

"Won't that kill the plant?"

"Don't put it directly in the pot. Just sprinkle it thickly around the outside like a castle moat. Trust me, it'll kill off any slug or snail that tries to climb up the side of the pot." He turned over a few leaves of the Tuscan cabbages, "if you are quick enough you will save them."

"Thank you, Mr Gordon, for such a wonderful idea," said Sandra happily. "

Mandy held her breath as she listened, for she knew there were small snails hidden in the deep crinkles of the leaves. She didn't want Mr Gordon to find them because they made silvery trails and had little horns which disappeared when she touched them. She let out her breath when Mr Gordon said:

"There is no sign of anything on these brassicas that I can see." He bent down and picked a slug off the paving stone and squished it between his thumb and fingers.

"What has made these holes then?" said Sandra, with a puzzled expression.

"Possibly a passing slug or beetle, let me get my glasses and I will have a better look."

"Why do you call the cabbages brassicas?" said Mandy. She grabbed his huge slug-squishing-hand and tugged him away from the pots.

"Brassica is the name for the whole cabbage family."

"So, is this a brassica?" asked Mandy, artfully pulling him towards the front door.

"No, that is a tomato," he said, looking at her strangely. He thought, what a stupid child not to know the difference between a tomato and a cabbage.

"Is this a cabbage?" Mandy opened her eyes wide as she pointed to a cucumber.

"Don't waste Mr Gordon's time with silly questions, Mandy," said Sandra, frowning at her daughter. "You know that is not a cabbage! Go and finish cleaning your room."

"Children will have their little jokes," said Mr Gordon, wiping the slime from his fingers on his trousers. He turned and wobbled away from the plants.

Mandy sighed with relief. Her plan had worked. Neither Mr Gordon nor her mother were looking for snails anymore. Once Mandy was gone, Sandra continued talking with her visitor.

"I was thinking about joining a gardening club, I thought it might be a way to make friends, what do you think, Mr Gordon?"

Mr Gordon rubbed his nose thoughtfully and looked troubled. "Well, you can…" he said slowly, "but I warn you, this is a hard town to break into if you are new. You have to be here thirty years before you are a local."

"Thirty years!" echoed Sandra, dismay in her voice. "Thirty years is a long time."

"That's the problem with a small town like this, it's run by a few ruling families who have lived here for generations. Have you got family within easy travelling distance?"

Sandra seemed to sag before Mr Gordon's eyes.

"No," she said sadly, "we are miles away from all our family and friends. I feel such an outsider here."

Mr Gordon felt sorry for her. "The A and P show is coming, enter something from your garden in it."

"What is the A and P show?"

"The Agricultural and Pastoral Show, of course."

When Sandra continued to look at him blankly, Mr Gordon slapped his leg and said, "you're having me on?"

"No, really," said Sandra, "I've always lived in big cities."

Mr Gordon stopped laughing and peered at her face. When he saw that she was not joking, he said: "Why, it is only the biggest thing that happens to this town all year. There are competitions for the best sheep, cows and pigs. Horse riding competitions, cake and pie competitions, flower and vegetable competitions. Everyone in the whole town enters something; even three-year-old's like this little one," he ruffled Billy's hair. "Mrs Young who is a hundred won the Christmas cake competition last year. It is the one weekend of the year nobody feels like an outsider."

Wendy Hamilton

Mandy and her pet snails.

The Britwhistles Win a Prize

A faraway look entered his eyes. "I wish I had Bruno; he'd win for sure." He sighed. "But that's life, you can't keep a bull in a retirement village."

"When is it held?" said Sandra, thinking it sounded fun.

"Very soon," said Mr Gordon, "if I were you, I'd dose your tomatoes with fertiliser and enter them. You can pick up an entry form from the post office." He looked at his watch. "Well, I must be going, all the best with your garden."

"Thank you so much, Mr Gordon," said Sandra waving.

As soon as he was out of sight, she went inside and picked up her shopping basket. "Get your shoes on kids," she called, as she pulled on a coat, "we are going for a walk."

"Where are we going?" said Mandy, coming out of her room.

Sandra helped Billy into his shoes and tied the laces, "we're going to the garden shop and the Post office."

Alfred's Apple-Faces

"Crazy, that's what they are," said Nelly to Molly. "I see smoke coming from their chimney all day."

Molly shook her head, "not crazy, just a little eccentric."

"Having a fire in this heat is more than eccentric," said Nelly. She picked up a nearby magazine and fanned her hot face with the Royal Family.

"That will be four dollars," said Molly, looking hard at Nelly. She felt good to be asserting herself for once. Nelly shop-soiled many things she never bought. "Are you interested in the Royal Wedding?"

"Four dollars! What a rip-off," said Nelly, stuffing the magazine back in the rack.

The Britwhistles Win a Prize

All week Mytle turned apples into applesauce.

Her thoughts swung back to the Britwhistles. "Cooking on a woodstove in this heat is a lot more than eccentric, it's plain crazy. They don't even have a telly."

"I don't think that is true," said Molly. "they have normal appliances, they just run them a different way."

"I'm telling you, they don't have a telly," insisted Nelly. "I was talking to Myrtle the other day and she knew nothing about Roger and Leanne's engagement!"

"Not everyone watches, 'When the Heart Churns', Nelly!"

"Everyone watches the news, Molly Tamworth," said Nelly, as if she was talking to someone extremely ignorant.

Molly threw up her hands. "Soap operas are not news."

"They are true to life," said Nelly. "There's a lot of good in Joanne. Last episode the police made a terrible mistake locking her in prison. They should have locked up Alfred Britwhistle instead."

"You shouldn't say things like that Nelly!"

Nelly tossed her head and snorted. "It's true, and what's more, next time he plays a trick on me I'm calling the police."

"Oh, I don't think you should do that, Alfred's

only playful. If you played a trick on him, he would love it. Why don't you pick something out of Boy's Corner? I've got a special on fake vomit this week."

"I would not stoop so low." Nelly glared at Molly. "You don't help the problem by selling him all that silly stuff. There ought to be a law against it."

Molly's face flushed. "What was it you came in for?"

"I can't remember. The service is so bad in this shop I've forgotten," Nelly said, stomping out.

"She only wanted to gossip," said Molly's husband as the door banged shut. "You're too soft. She keeps coming here because you let her go on and on."

Molly wiped her hand over her eyes. "I know." There was a small pause and suddenly her face brightened. "I stood up to her over the magazine though."

Wilbur nodded approvingly. "That was a step in the right direction."

"And I cut her gossip short. Fancy saying they should put dear old Alfred in prison!"

"Don't let her get you down. I wonder what that old couple are up to, cooking all day in this heat?"

"Oh Wilbur, trust a man not to know. Don't you remember all the preserving jars Mrs B. bought last week? It's bottling season!"

"What will she be preserving?"

"Apples probably. I hope Alfred doesn't decide to play another trick on Nelly in the next few days, apples are just the sort of things Alfred might decide to have fun with."

Molly had guessed correctly on both accounts. Alfred spent all Monday picking apples and plotting his next joke. On Tuesday morning, once Myrtle was safely in the kitchen peeling apples, Alfred went out to his workshop with a grin on his face. Sitting on his workbench were the six big apples he had put aside the day before. Rubbing his hands together gleefully, he picked up the first apple.

"Let's see how this goes," he murmured to himself. He plunged an apple corer into the apple and pulled out the core. Then, whistling gently through his teeth, he pushed a small test tube into the hole. It slid in easily and disappeared into the centre of the apple. "Perfect, now for the others."

When all six apples were done, Alfred took out his pocketknife and started carving the biggest one. As he cut, the tip of his tongue stuck out. It took some time, but at last he put the apple down. "A pretty good face, even if I do say so myself," he said, looking at it with pride. "Every bit as good as a Halloween pumpkin. Now for the eyes." He selected two gobstoppers from a nearby jar, gouged out eye sockets, and forced the sweets into them. The face, once he finished drawing spirals on the eyeballs, was as hideous as he hoped. So awful, Alfred was disappointed he couldn't show it to Myrtle. By the time the lunch gong rang he had carved all the apples into faces. He covered them with a sack and went inside.

"What have you been up to this morning?" said Myrtle, putting a meat pie on the table.

Alfred went red and avoided his wife's gaze. "I've thought up a way to turn baking soda into pellets."

Myrtle poured two cups of tea. "That's nice, Love, what do you use them for?"

"What do I use them for? That's a good question. What are they for?" stalled Alfred, trying to think of a convincing reason. "They will be good because they won't make such a mess as powder when you cook." The words came out in a rush.

"That's very nice of you to think of me. Are you alright, Dear?" said Myrtle, looking at him with a worried expression, "your face has gone all red."

Alfred pulled a large spotted handkerchief from his pocket and mopped his forehead. "Just the heat of the kitchen, Love, nothing to fret about."

"It is rather hot," said Myrtle, her face relaxing.

"The stove does heat up the kitchen. Only a few more hours before the apple sauce is cooked."

Alfred, putting his hanky back in his pocket, replied without thinking, "good, that leaves enough time."

"Leaves enough time for what?"

Alfred, realizing his mistake, coughed awkwardly and said, "for making the baking soda pellets."

"Are you sure you are alright, Dear?" Myrtle's forehead creased into worry lines. "You haven't been eating lots of little sour apples again, have you?"

"Of course not," growled Alfred, "I tell you, there is nothing wrong with me. My mind is just busy inventing at the moment."

Myrtle's forehead smoothed out. "Oh, that's all right then."

She chatted about the apple sauce while Alfred gobbled his pie hurriedly. As soon as lunch was over, he took a jar of baking soda, a tray, and a bottle of vinegar from the pantry and scarpered back to his workshop.

"I didn't tell a lie," he said to the cat as he put the things on the bench, "the pellets will be less messy than powder." But he had not told the complete truth either, because once he had made six pellets he pushed the baking soda aside and poured a tablespoon of vinegar into the middle of each apple-head. Then he put them on the tray and crept out the door.

There was no sign of Nelly when Alfred swung a couple of loose boards aside and squeezed through the fence. Keeping his head low, he crept across the driveway and along the side of the house until he was under Nelly's kitchen window. He heard the television blaring, so he raised his head cautiously. Nelly, in the adjoining room, sat in an armchair with her back to him. Grinning, Alfred lined the apples along the windowsill so they faced into the kitchen. Then he popped a pellet in each test tube, before scampering back home. As he expected, it did not take long for the pellets to dissolve in the vinegar. He stood on the steps of his workshop with his fingers on the string of his whistle as he stared over the fence. When large plumes of mist puffed out the top of each apple-head, he pulled down hard.

"Shrieeeeeeeek screamed the whistle. The sound was so loud, Nelly leapt to her feet and ran to the window to see what the noise was. Her squeal when she saw the apple-faces grinning at her was as good as Alfred hoped. He was bent over and roaring with laughter when Nelly's head jerked above the top of the fence. The sinews of her neck stood out and her mouth was a thin line as she shook her fist at him and shouted:

"I've had it with you, Alfred Britwhistle, I'm calling the police." And then she hurled an apple-head at him, stomped back to her house, and slammed the door.

Myrtle Makes a Bear

The day after the apple incident was Wednesday, the day the patchwork club met, and Myrtle was telling the ladies about Alfred's apple prank.

"It was so embarrassing. I was making apple sauce in the kitchen when I heard someone pounding on the front door, and when I opened it, there was Nelly with a policeman and an arm-full of awful apple-heads. I don't know what gets into Alfred sometimes?"

"Oh my," said Maud Moody.

"Dear oh dear," said Agnes Brumby. Her head wobbled between sips from her rose teacup. They were still at the tea stage of the proceedings, "how dreadful!"

Myrtle put her cup on her saucer and leant forward. "Nelly wanted Alfred charged for disturbing the peace!"

The ladies shook their heads gently and murmured, "dear dear, shocking shocking," in soothing tones.

"Fortunately, the policeman was a lovely young man," Myrtle reached for a cucumber sandwich. She was about to take a bite when a new thought hit her. "I think he might be one of Hilda's sons because he is a Jefferson."

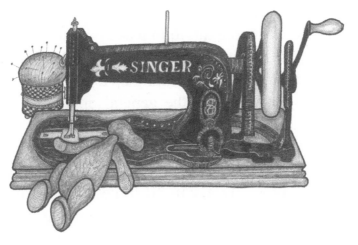

"That will be Tony," Mrs Jennings nodded. "He's the third boy. I remember he was training to be a policeman a few years ago."

The Britwhistles Win a Prize

"A lovely boy," echoed Edna Golding, taking a polite bite of chocolate cake.

"As I was saying," said Myrtle, swallowing, "Nelly wanted him arrested for disturbing the peace. But what noise do apples make?" she asked, looking around indignantly.

All the ladies (except Mrs Grundy) shook their heads in sympathy and made small clicking noises with their tongues.

"Then Tony," (Myrtle knew his name now) "said he didn't think the apples were disturbing anyone's peace. But she said, get this, that they were disturbing her peace and the way they grinned at her was offensive."

There was more tut, tutting as sympathy poured over Myrtle for having a neighbour like Nelly.

"Good on Tony for standing up to her," said Mrs Jennings, who voiced the general opinion of the room.

Myrtle, starting to feel a bit better, sat up straighter. "I do wish Alfred wouldn't wind her up," she said, drooping again. "It turned out alright in the end; apart from the apple sauce boiling over. I suspect Tony thought it was rather funny. Alfred's apple-heads, not the mess in the kitchen I mean, because his mouth kept turning up and down as if he was trying not to laugh; especially when a gobstopper fell out of one of the apples. Even so, the whole thing was very embarrassing. I usually get on with my neighbours but... Nelly is so difficult and Alfred is naughty at times."

"I don't know why we are talking about Nelly. She is not my neighbour," cut in Mrs Grundy loudly. There was a sudden silence apart from a few uncomfortable shuffling noises. "We are here to discuss our new project. Has anyone come up with an idea?"

Mrs Golding cleared her throat. "I suppose you have all been watching the bushfires in Victoria on the TV."

The ladies nodded.

"It's so sad," she said, "all these people have lost everything. I know we always send quilts in sympathy, but what about making something different for the children? I feel so sorry for them losing all their toys."

At this, the Patched-Up ladies looked a little weepy.

"I think Teddy bears are so comforting." Edna's voice wobbled as she dabbed at her eyes. "I found these patterns in the library and I thought you might like to have a look at them." Her fingers trembled slightly as she passed a thick book to Mrs Grundy. Myrtle, Mrs Jennings, Mrs Moody, and Millicent

The Britwhistles Win a Prize

Mable held their breath and looked at the queen bee. Mrs Grundy glanced through the book and closed her eyes. Her eyebrows lifted and her eyelashes fluttered while she thought about the proposed idea. At last, she slowly opened her eyes and said:

"I think the idea has merit."

Permission granted, an excited buzz filled the room as the women (all talking at once) gathered around the book. Myrtle was the last to choose a pattern. Most of the bears did not appeal to her. Then, just when she thought she would have to make an ordinary bear, she saw the right one. He was smaller than the others and had a longer snout; he wore a knitted cardigan and peered at her from beady black eyes.

"What are they made of?" she asked, pleased with her choice.

"Fake fur, but unfortunately that kind of fabric is quite expensive, so I was thinking of making them out of old coats," replied Mrs Golding, looking at Mrs Grundy again.

Myrtle thought of her coat in the back of the wardrobe. "There is my old brown coat, Alfred cut a hole in it, would that do?"

"What do you think Mrs. Grundy?" asked Edna.

"I think that would be satisfactory," said Mrs Grundy. "I have some balls of wool I can donate for the knitted garments," she added graciously.

Now that Mrs Grundy had given the nod of approval to used coats, everyone felt free to discuss all the old coats in her wardrobe.

"I've got a blue mohair coat I could spare," said Millicent Mable, looking at Mrs Grundy. "The moths got into the collar. Do you think a blue bear would be alright though?" She nibbled her fingernails as she waited for the answer.

"Quite alright," said Mrs Grundy, "I shall be making a pink bear."

That settled, the day swung along very merrily, and before the afternoon was over every woman had taken a copy of the pattern she liked, and promised to make six bears for the poor bush fire children.

All the next week Myrtle's scissors went snip snip and her sewing machine went clickety-clack. When all the snip snipping and clackety clacking was finished, the snickity-snickering started as Myrtle's knitting needles flew in and out. Finally, all the snipping and clacking and snickering stopped, and there sat six little brown bears, each one wearing a brightly coloured cardigan. Myrtle arranged them in a long row on the mantelpiece, pulled a rocking chair in front of the fire and sat down to admire them. They were very smiley bears, Myrtle felt proud of them. She stared at them as she rocked back and forth, and the longer she stared the more she loved them, and the more she loved them, the more difficult it was to part with them; even for sad children who had lost all their toys in bush fires.

"What shall I do?" said Myrtle to Alfred, when he came in for his cup of tea. "I don't want to part with any of my bears, but a grown woman doesn't need one bear, let alone six!"

Alfred was not interested in the bears, but he hid his feelings and took the matter seriously.

"I think, Myrtle, you should make two more bears and keep the best ones for Sally and Peter to play with when they come."

"What a wonderful idea, you are such a clever man," said Myrtle, smiling. "I won't choose which ones I'll keep until I have made them all." And she stood up and went straight off to make two more bears.

Myrtle's bears had been getting better with each bear she made, but the last bear was vastly better. Although she cut him from the same pattern, and there was nothing particularly stunning about his red cardigan, there was just something about the expression around his mouth, and his little bead-eyes looked so sad, it melted your heart.

"He seems almost alive," said Mrs Moody in a tone of wonder. It was Wednesday again and the ladies of the sewing group were clustered around Myrtle's bear.

"You certainly have a knack for making bears," said Mrs Jennings. She also had a tone of surprise in her voice, but for a different reason, for while Myrtle had made many beautiful quilts, none of them were up to competition standard. Myrtle had never won a ribbon at the A and P show, although she entered every year.

"The show has a category for dolls and bears this year," said Millicent Mable so nervously, she sounded as if she was apologising. "I suppose it is a stupid idea, but I thought maybe, just possibly, Mrs B might enter the Best Bear competition. What do you think, Mrs. Grundy?"

Mrs Grundy's eyes closed and stayed shut much longer than usual because it was a new idea. Eventually, she nodded her head like the Queen and said:

"Mrs Britwhistle may enter her bear."

At the end of the day Myrtle almost floated home, she was so happy. "Alfred, Alfred," she called as she burst through the workshop door, "the ladies think I should enter this bear in the A and P show." She held out one of the two bears in her hands. "There is a bear class this year and they think I have a chance of winning."

The Britwhistles Win a Prize

The bear in the hutch-dresser .

Alfred put down the piece of wood he was sanding and looked at his wife.

"That's wonderful, Love."

"I do so want to win a prize. I've never won a prize."

"Yes, you have, you won a certificate for the most improved quilter one year."

"Oh, Honey, that doesn't count," said Myrtle, "it's not the same thing as a blue ribbon. You can be the worst at anything and also the most improved."

Alfred nodded. "I suppose that's true."

Myrtle did a clumsy little twirl and her thick orthopaedic shoes squeaked on the floor.

"I can't wait to enter him in the show."

"Well, you won't have to wait long, it's only a few weeks away. I'm guessing these are the two bears you are keeping."

"Yes, they are," said Myrtle, "I'm keeping the best one for Sally and giving the second-best bear to Peter, because Sally likes bears more than Peter does."

"Good idea," said Alfred. He picked up his wood again and rubbed a piece of sandpaper back and forth along the grain.

Myrtle saw he wanted to get on with his work, so she hobbled back down the path to the house. She was so excited over her bear, she mounted the stairs without dread, and hummed as she put the second-best bear on Peter's bed. She did not put the best bear on Sally's bed, however, because sometimes the cat sat there. Instead, she put him in the hutch-dresser.

Mandy has Trouble

In the show grounds at the edge of town men bustled about pitching tents, setting up sideshows and marking out parking areas. The field was not the only place of activity. On every farm and in every house and schoolroom, people were getting their exhibits ready. The kids were especially excited because they got Friday off to go to the show. Everyone, from the new entrance babies to the big kids, had something to enter. Even Mandy's little brother Billy had drawn a picture. He did it in green and purple crayon and was supposed to be a duck and a dog.

"Anyone with half an eye could see it was hideous," Mandy told Jane as they walked home from school, "but Mum and I pretended it was

115

wonderful, and told him he was a clever boy."

"Have you made your sand garden yet?" asked Jane, "I've got the sand in my saucer but I don't know what to plant."

"Weren't you listening at school? You don't plant things in a saucer garden," said Mandy, "you arrange flowers on top of the sand so they look pretty."

"You don't have to sound like my mother!" said Jane, frowning.

"I've made a really beautiful one that I'm keeping a secret in case someone copies me. I'll let you see it though because you're my best friend," said Mandy, linking arms with her.

"What's it like?" asked Jane, accepting the apology.

"I've a lovely red rose in the middle and around it I've got purple, yellow and white circles of daisies, violets, and strawflowers."

Jane swung her schoolbag as they wandered along. "Sounds really nice. What are you going to call it?"

"Rose's Glory," said Mandy, "I wanted a romantic name because it looks like a rose radiating ripples of glory." (By now they had got to Mandy's house.) "Come in a see it."

"Alright, but only for a little while, I've still

got my garden to make, and they have to be in tomorrow."

Sandra was kneeling beside her tomato plant trying to decide which were the best tomatoes as they walked down the front path. Billy, nearby, was shooting tin cans off the fence with a bow and arrow.

"Hello, Mrs Bloomingdale," said Jane politely as they walked past.

"Hello, Jane," said Sandra, getting up hastily and smoothing her hair behind her ears.

"I'm going to show Jane my sand garden," said Mandy, slinging her schoolbag through the open door.

"Mandy Dear," Sandra twisted the corner of her gardening apron nervously, "I need to talk to you about that, there's been a little accident."

"What kind of accident?" asked Mandy suspiciously.

"I bought Billy a bow and arrow this afternoon to keep him occupied while I got ready for the show," said Sandra, glancing towards Billy who was stalking the cucumbers, "unfortunately, he thought your sand garden looked like a target."

Mandy's face crumpled into dismay. "You don't mean to tell me he shot it?" she said in horrified tones.

The Britwhistles Win a Prize

Sandra wrung her hands. "I'm so sorry Dear, I know the garden means a lot to you, he hasn't done much damage."

Mandy rushed inside and Sandra followed her.

"He's ruined it," shouted Mandy when she saw it. "He's shot the rose!"

"I expect he thought it was the bullseye," said Sandra.

"Well, at least the rest of the garden is alright," said Mandy, calming down a little, "I'll swap this for another rose." She was about to remove it from the saucer, but her mother caught her hand.

"It's not as simple as that, Honey, I had the same idea, but he has shot all the roses off the bushes."

"Oh no," wailed Mandy, "my life is over, I can't go to school with a garden like that."

Jane, who was feeling uncomfortable, sidled towards the door. "I've got to go now Mandy, I'm sorry about your rose, I'll see you tomorrow."

"Ok," nodded Mandy. She was pleased to see Jane go because she did not want to burst into tears in front of her.

"When life gives you a lemon, make lemonade out of it," said her mother, patting Mandy's shoulder as the door banged behind Jane.

"What do you mean make lemonade?" said Mandy looking tragic. "He's ruined my garden, and my teacher told us we have to hand them in tomorrow morning."

"We can't fix it the way you want it fixed, but we can do something with it. Let's leave the arrow in and make it look like it's meant to be there." Sandra took a small card and wrote (in the fancy writing she only used for party invitations) 'My Best Shot by Mandy Bloomingdale.' "There," she said, "you have to call your entry something. This will make the arrow look like part of the design."

It was a good idea and the card looked very professional. Nobody else's mother had such nice handwriting. Mandy sniffed and wiped her eyes.

"Thanks, Mum," she said. She felt better about the disaster now, at least she had something to hand in tomorrow. But in the morning when she saw all the other sand gardens, Mandy felt the tears welling up again.

"This is going to look ridiculous amongst all the pretty sand gardens. The only other one that looks as stupid as mine is Lottie Ashworth's one," said Mandy, as she and Jane gazed at a saucer covered with tiny cactuses.

Jane tilted her head to one side and read the name of Lottie's sand garden aloud. "'Just Deserts.' I suppose the name is a play on words." She giggled, "Her garden is as sharp as her tongue."

The Britwhistles Win a Prize

Mandy was too upset to laugh. "It's humiliating to think the whole town will know I've made something as stupid as the least popular girl in the school."

The school bell rang.

"Perhaps you could drop your garden and say it was an accident," said Jane, putting her saucer next to 'Fairy Garden.'

"I thought of that but then I would lose marks for not completing my project," said Mandy pulling a face as she plunked, My Best Shot, next to 'Heaven's Glade.' "I wish it would get lost!"

"Who's in charge of getting everything to the show?" asked Jane with a glimmer of hope.

"Mr Nugent!" said Mandy gloomily.

"Oh!" said Jane. They walked to class silently. The whole way there Jane wanted to say something encouraging, but she couldn't think of anything. Everyone knew Mr Nugent was very efficient.

The Britwhistles get ready for the show

It was the day before the show and Alfred was in his garden. It was a slow business choosing the best produce. He went up and down each row of vegetables seven times before making any decisions. Myrtle was doing a similar thing in the kitchen among the shelves where her preserves sat. At last she chose two bottles of apple sauce before going into the front room and opening a blanket box. The box was where she kept her best quilts. She pulled out several and put them on Alfred's wingback chair.

"This one, this one, but not this one," she

said, looking at the seams of each quilt through a magnifying glass. When she finished, she opened the glass door of the hutch dresser and took out her best bear.

"Oh, my, you have got dusty," she said, whisking a clothes'-brush over him. She held him up to the light and inspected him closely. "With a bit of luck, you will be a winner by the end of the weekend," she said, putting him on top of the pile of quilts.

As she spoke Alfred came in carrying a huge blue-grey pumpkin.

"Look at this beauty, Myrtle," he said. "Maybe I will get another cup this year."

"Goodness, that is a big one. I reckon you stand a good chance."

"I've got a whopper marrow and some excellent tomatoes as well."

"How are we going to get all this stuff to the show now we can't drive Lulu?" said Myrtle with a puzzled crease on her brow.

"I think the best idea is to use the wheelbarrow for my veggies, and Baxter for your stuff," said Alfred. "I pulled her out of the woodshed before I came in. She's a bit dusty and her tires need pumping up, but other than that, she's fine."

"What a good idea," said Myrtle, following him out to the woodshed.

Wendy Hamilton

Alfred choosing his best vegetables.

The Britwhistles Win a Prize

She looked at Baxter with a worried frown. "I hope I can remember how to ride a bike."

"Of course, you can," Alfred said breezily. "It's impossible to forget how to ride a bike."

"I hope you're right." Myrtle still looked doubtful. "If I have too much trouble I could always push her, I suppose," she added, brightening up. "The basket is perfect."

"They don't make baskets like this anymore," said Alfred, smacking the metal frame that held a large rectangular basket. "I knew as soon as I saw her a delivery bike would come in handy someday."

Myrtle laughed and poked his arm playfully. "Ten years is a long time to wait for something to become handy, you need to stop going to auctions, Alfie."

"Baxter's Bakery is useful," said Alfred, speaking as if the words on the sign under the seat were the bike's full name. "I keep all the leftover paint in her." As he spoke, he pointed at a heap of paint tins by the woodshed.

Myrtle scrubbed a black stain with her handkerchief. "And oil by the look of it. I don't want any of this to come off onto my quilts."

"Hang on a minute," said Alfred, disappearing into his workshop. When he returned, he was carrying a sheet of clear plastic. "Here you go. This will keep everything clean." He spread it over the bottom of the basket.

"That'll work," said Myrtle, pleased. "There's enough to go right over the top as well. I might need it. The weather forecast for Sunday is rain."

"I don't mind if it rains," said Alfred, "so long as it doesn't rain tomorrow. I will have done all the rides by Sunday."

"That's all very well, but I don't want to get wet when we take everything home again."

"Don't worry about it, Myrtle. Go and get your things ready while I pump up the tires. The weatherman may be wrong, he often is."

"Here's hoping," said Myrtle, walking back towards the house. She went into the front room and scooped up the bear along with the quilts. As she passed through the kitchen on her way out again, she grabbed the preserves, and carried everything out to the bike by the woodshed. Then she put the bottles of applesauce into Baxter's basket, and the quilts on top of the bottles, and the bear on top of the quilts. She heard the rumbling of a metal wheel on the brick path as she worked, and shortly Alfred rounded the corner of the shed with his wooden wheelbarrow.

"I'm all set to go, are you ready Myrtle?" he asked.

The Britwhistles Win a Prize

"Nearly, I've just got to cover this," said Myrtle. "I don't want anything falling out. You go on ahead and I'll catch you up."

"Cheerio then, I'll see you soon," said Alfred. And with that, he rumbled down the driveway and away.

The sound of the wheelbarrow faded as Myrtle spread a plastic sheet over everything and tucked it down tight. When she finished, she put her right foot on the highest peddle.

"Here I go," she said, as she stood down hard on it. As the peddle swung down and the bike moved forward, Myrtle hopped about on her other foot until she managed to get both feet on the peddles. "Oh my, I might not have forgotten how to ride a bike, but I sure am rusty," she said, as she wibble-wobbled around the side of the house, through a lavender bush, and over the cat's tail.

"Sorry Marmaduke," she called over her shoulder as he hissed at her.

Now she was on the bike, Myrtle had a new problem; she was not sure how to stop. She zig-zagged along the road, rode slowly up a hill and whizzed terrifyingly down the other side. At length, she arrived at her destination and Myrtle (suddenly remembering where the brakes were) dismounted Baxter clumsily.

"You took your time," said Alfred. "I thought you would have caught up to me ages ago."

"It's a miracle I got here at all," said Myrtle, wheeling Baxter towards a string of buildings where the exhibits were. Alfred turned left and trundled his wheelbarrow into an enormous room for produce and flowers, while Myrtle turned right and wheeled her bike into an enormous room for sewing and cooking.

It was just as busy inside as outside. People bustled about as they flipped open trestle tables and set up booths. Overhead an electrician strung up lights, while another man ran cables along the floor, and the ham-man trundled his big wooden churn for spinning raffle tickets next to a microphone. Myrtle, ignoring the shouts, bangs, and the thrum of a generator, pushed Baxter towards the quilt and doll section. Already many quilts hung from the wooden stands laid out in long rows. Across from the quilts were hay bales piled into shelves. Porcelain dolls of all sizes stood on the hay, and at the end of the porcelain dolls, was a section for bears. Myrtle flicked the bike stand out and leaned Baxter onto it.

"Oh my, I never expected so many bears," she said to the woman in charge of registration as she took her bear out from under the plastic cover.

The Britwhistles Win a Prize

At length they arrived at their destination.

The woman gave a brief nod. She had short grey hair and wore a flowing black top splashed with blobs of colour. Around her neck dangled a necklace of chunky plastic beads that looked like sucked sweets. She sat at a portable table and her broad bottom, in stretchy black pants, oozed over the sides of a small canvas chair.

"Name and address?"

"Myrtle Britwhistle, three Station Road, Woolomaloo."

The woman bent over a receipt book and the table shook as she wrote everything down. When she had finished, she swivelled the book around and handed Myrtle a pen. "We take no responsibility for theft or damage to the exhibits. Sign here," she said in a monotone. Myrtle signed her name while the woman picked a number out of a box on the table. "Pin this on your exhibit and give it to Pricilla," she said, handing Myrtle a disk with a small safety pin in it.

Myrtle looked confused as she pinned fifty-five onto her bear. "Who is Pricilla?"

"The woman wearing the hat."

Myrtle looked around and saw a thin woman in a flowery hat. She wore a floral dress and was fluffing about arranging bears artistically.

"I'm to give this to you," said Myrtle, handing

her the bear.

"Thank you," said the thin woman taking him. A pair of glasses hung from a chain around her neck like a sink plug. She picked them up and examined the bear closely. "He's a little cutie, isn't he Norma?"

"Yes, he is," said the sucked-sweets woman, looking at Myrtle's exhibit properly for the first time. The thin woman, still holding the bear turned to compliment Myrtle. But she had disappeared into the maze of quilts.

Competitions

It was the first day of the show and Alfred was having a lovely time. He rode the merry-go-round six times, the Ferris wheel four times, and the hurricane twice. He even managed to get Myrtle on the rollercoaster; which required great cunning and trickery. He was wandering through the livestock tent eating a hotdog, when a large man wearing a suit and smoking a cigar called out to him.

"Well, if it isn't Alfred Britwhistle!"

"Herbert Popple, is it really you?"

"It is indeed."

"It's been a long time," said Alfred, sticking his hand out.

"Too long," said Herbert, grasping Alfred's hand and shaking it. "Last time we met we had hair. Won any marble games lately, Alfie," he chuckled.

"I don't go in for marbles anymore."

Herbert leaned back and blew a smoke ring, "just as well, I always bet you."

"No, you didn't."

"Your memory is getting shaky in your old age, Son," said Herbert, slapping Alfred on the back heartily. "I bet you in marbles, maths, spelling, cricket, you name it, I bet you."

"What have you been up to?" said Alfred, changing the subject.

"I sold used cars when I left school and did very well. Now I own car yards all over Australia. What about you Alfie, I suppose you are still tinkering with Bunsen burners and chemistry sets."

"Well, yes," admitted Alfred feeling small, "I got into Alternate Energy and worked in Sydney until I retired and shifted here."

"You don't mean to tell me you live in this hole in the sticks! Oh well, we can't all be top of the tree," said Herbert, slapping Alfred on the back again.

It was a pity they were still in the livestock tent, because if they had been somewhere else Alfred would not have seen the competition.

"Hey Herbert, I bet you can't guess the weight of this."

Herbert blew another smoke ring and replied lazily, "it's a waste of time competing with me Alfred, I always win."

"You're just scared," taunted Alfred.

Herbert's face went red and he ground his cigar on the top of a fence post. "I am not!" he said, throwing the butt on the ground.

"Go on then."

"All right," said Herbert, "and I bet you afternoon tea, I'll win."

"You're on!" said Alfred, climbing into the pen.

It was clever of Alfred to win. Two-hundred-and-fifty others had tried for the prize, but Alfred's guess was the closest. It did help that he picked the goat up and felt its weight in his arms. Nobody else dared to do that. He was glorying in his triumph as he ate a large slice of cake, when Herbert popped his bubble of joy.

"So, what will the wife think about your prize, Alf?"

Alfred's fork dropped from his fingers and clattered on the plate. "We should have gone in for guessing lollies in the jar instead," he said, shaking his head.

"No, I think you picked the right one, Son, I couldn't think of a competition I would rather lose," said Herbert, pulling a fat wallet from his pocket and paying the bill.

It was a relief when Alfred's old friend departed in a cloud of smoke rings. Even a small amount of Herbert was depressing. A few rides on the Hurricane, however, restored Alfred's mood. He was wandering about in a haze of happiness, eating a wad of pink candy floss on a stick, when a woman in high heels, a tight short skirt, and carrying a clipboard stepped in front of him.

"Yooooo whoooooo Mr Britwhistle."

"Oh, hello Mrs Drummond," said Alfred, coming out of his happy haze. Nobody could stay in a happy haze when Mrs Drummond was around. At least, it wasn't wise to. Mrs Drummond was an organiser and you might end up with ten jobs if you were not alert.

"Mr Britwhistle, I thought you might help me out with a teensy-weensy little job."

"Oh," said Alfred nervously. He had not finished all the rides yet and did not want to find himself in the tea tent washing dishes all afternoon.

"Mrs Vernon was to judge the under-tens sand garden exhibits, but she can't make it; some silly excuse about breaking her leg. I feel very let down but then I saw you and I thought, Alfred Britwhistle would make the perfect replacement."

"I suppose so," said Alfred, looking at the ice-cream stand longingly. "When do I do it?"

"Now, follow me," said Mrs Drummond, tottering over to the exhibition building.

Alfred clumped after her with his head down and his hands in his pocket. When they got to the sand garden booth Mrs Drummond handed him the clipboard.

"Here we are," she said, "the gardens are all numbered, just write first, second, and third, next to the numbers you choose and hand it in at the office. Got to fly, tat-tar." She waved and disappeared.

The sand garden booth was bursting with gardens. Alfred's head went dizzy with all the colours and patterns. There were two, however, that stood out and took his fancy. One looked like a target with an arrow in it, while cactuses covered the other. It was a hard choice. He liked the bright colours of the target and he loved bows and arrows...... but then....... the biggest cactus was fascinating. It bristled with needles so fine it looked hairy.

I wonder if it spits needles? He thought. He put his hand close to it and discovered it did.

"Definitely worth first prize," he muttered to himself, as he sucked prickles from his finger. "But then, so is the target, in an entirely different way." He chuckled as he looked at it. It was as bright as a traffic light, and the arrow rammed in the rose made him laugh. He stood there for a long time with his pen hovering between two numbers, uncertain which to choose.

Wendy Hamilton

Myrtle's bear Wins a Prize

If Mandy thought for one moment someone was thinking about giving her garden a prize she would have been astonished; as it was, it never crossed her mind because she and Jane were having too much fun. They had ten dollars to spend as they liked. They spent two dollars on the ghost train, which wasn't worth it, two dollars on the roller coaster, which made up for it, two dollars on a bag of candy floss they shared, and two dollars on a hotdog each. By early afternoon, the money was all gone, so they drifted from the sideshows to the exhibition building. The exhibitions were free to look at and there was plenty to see, so they took their time.

The Britwhistles Win a Prize

"I wish he was my bear," said Mandy to Jane.

Jane's favourite stall was the porcelain dolls, but Mandy's was the Teddy bears. There was one bear in particular. He was small and sat right in the middle, with his arm slightly raised as if he was waving. His sad little eyes tugged at Mandy's heartstrings, and she thought he was the best bear by far. The judges agreed, because pinned to his red cardigan was a blue ribbon. She pointed him out to Jane and said wistfully, "I wish he was my bear."

"Would you? I would rather have a porcelain doll," said Jane, glancing at him indifferently. "I'm sick of hanging around here. I want to see if my sand garden has won anything."

"Oh alright," said Mandy, tearing herself away from the appealing bear. She went slowly and reluctantly because even the thought of her exhibit made her feel embarrassed. "You go on ahead. I want to look at the vegetables first." She did not think her mother's tomato was good enough to win a prize; she only said it to delay going near the sand gardens.

As expected, Sandra's tomato had not won anything. It was small compared to the winning tomato, and its mottled colour wasn't good either. Mandy was looking at an enormous pumpkin and wondering how to grow one that big when Jane came running up to her.

The Britwhistles Win a Prize

"You've won first prize!" she blurted out.

"Don't be silly, I can't have."

"You have, and Lottie's second! Come and see," said Jane, grabbing her arm and dragging her over to the sand gardens.

It was true. Mandy could hardly believe her eyes. There was a blue ribbon stuck on the saucer of 'My Best Shot.'

Myrtle and Alfred were sauntering past the sand garden booth as Mandy and Jane jumped about in excitement.

"That was very nice of you to help out with the judging, Honey. You've made someone very happy," said Myrtle, looking at the girls.

"She did better than I did," said Alfred, "I thought I might at least get a merit certificate for my pumpkin."

"Never mind, you can't win something every year."

"I didn't say I hadn't won anything," muttered Alfred.

"What do you mean? They have finished all the judging."

Alfred coughed awkwardly and changed the subject. "Have you looked to see if you've had any success?"

"No, I never do, so I haven't bothered looking."

"Well, you might be in for a bit of a surprise this time."

"Really?" said Myrtle in an excited tone.

"Come with me," said Alfred, hustling her into the next room and over to the bear section.

"I can't believe it," said Myrtle (although she certainly did) "my first blue ribbon!"

"Isn't it wonderful," said Alfred. He was very happy for his wife. Moreover, he was pleased that in her excitement she had forgotten about his mysterious prize.

Myrtle's eyes were shining and she clasped her hands together in delight. "I've won a prize," she kept saying over and over.

"You certainly have and it's well-deserved," said Alfred putting his arm around her shoulders.

It rained as the weatherman predicted, but by the time Alfred and Myrtle collected their exhibits at the end of the show, it had eased off.

Alfred, watching Myrtle tuck her bear down the edge of Baxter's basket said;

"If it starts raining again, he'll get wet."

"I'll pack him under the plastic if it starts spitting," said Myrtle, arranging the bear so his head and arms were visible, "but until then I want everyone to see I've won a ribbon."

The Britwhistles Win a Prize

"Before we go home," said Alfred, looking down and shuffling his feet, "I've got to collect my prize."

"So there really is a prize? I thought it was just a load of nonsense."

"No, there really is."

"Well, what is it?"

"You'll see, just follow me." He grasped the handles of his wheelbarrow and rumbled to the far side of the showground and over to the livestock tent.

"Leave Baxter here," he said, putting the wheelbarrow down. He picked up a length of rope that Myrtle had not noticed before. She flicked out the bike stand, leaned Baxter onto it and followed him, growing more and more puzzled as he opened the flap of the tent and walked over to the man in charge.

"Ah, Alfred," said the man, "I'm glad you've come for your prize. You've got a rope, I see, very good. I'll be back in a moment." He took the rope and disappeared into a stall at the far end of the tent.

Myrtle heard a great deal of thumping and banging and bleating, and eventually the man reappeared, dragging a Billy goat behind him.

"What is that?" said Myrtle. It was a silly thing to say because she knew perfectly well what it was.

"It's my prize," said Alfred in a small voice. "I won it by guessing its weight."

"I don't believe it!" said Myrtle. They were the same words she said when she saw the blue ribbon on her bear, but her tone was completely different. "What on earth are we going to do with a Billy goat? We can't even milk him."

"I thought we could put him in the paddock behind the garden to keep the weeds down," said Alfred lamely.

"Humph," said Myrtle. It was not a friendly sound. "Can't we say we don't want your prize?"

"I already have. But they said I have to take it. I didn't realise when I signed the entry form that I was agreeing to keep him if I won him."

"Well, I suppose we will just have to make the best of it," sighed Myrtle, "I have only myself to blame, I should not have let you out of my sight."

All the time they were talking, Alfred was dragging the goat behind him. It wasn't like walking a dog; it was more like dragging a cat on a lead, only stiffer and bigger. When they got outside the tent, he tied the end of the rope onto the carrier behind Baxter's seat.

"Oh no, don't even think about it!" said Myrtle, glaring at him.

"You'll have to, I can't take it."

"Why not?"

"Because I need both my hands for the wheelbarrow."

"If you think I'm going to drag that goat all through the village, you have another think coming. I'll push the wheelbarrow and you can take the bike with the stinking goat."

The idea might have worked if the wheelbarrow was empty. But loaded as it was with monstrous vegetables, it was too heavy. Even so, Myrtle staggered a few steps before she admitted defeat.

"You'll be alright it's not that far," Alfred encouraged, as his wife reluctantly agreed to tow the goat. "I've had an idea that I think might work." He fished about in his pocket until he found the piece of string he always carried. Then he grabbed a big bunch of carrots from the wheelbarrow and tied them onto the bike carrier.

"Here you go, goaty," he said, snapping a bit off the biggest carrot. He waved it under the goat's nose. "Plenty more over here," he said, moving the carrot from the goat to the bike and back several times before giving it to him. The horizontal slit in the yellow eyes looked at the bunch of carrots with interest and he licked his lips.

"He's got the idea, get on the bike Myrtle. I'll push him to get him going."

"It's my prize," said Alfred in a small voice.

The Britwhistles Win a Prize

Alfred's idea worked, but not brilliantly; the journey home was difficult and took a long time. Sometimes the goat would run at the carrots and butt the back of the bike with his head. Other times he would stop dead in his tracks and jerk the bike backwards. With so much going on behind her, Myrtle gave scant attention to the basket in front, even when the handlebars flicked sideways, or the wheel banged against the gutter.

"It's a miracle I haven't fallen off Baxter yet," grumbled Myrtle, as she struggled to stay upright.

"We'll be home soon, it's not much further," said Alfred, as he trudged behind her pushing the wheelbarrow, "and when we get there I will make you a nice cup of tea, and you can sit in front of the fire and admire your blue ribbon."

"I'd like that," said Myrtle.

It is a pity that neither she nor Alfred glanced at the basket, for if they had, they might have seen her prize bear topple out of the basket. As it was, they were so preoccupied they did not see him fall to the ground, or the dog that picked him up and carried him away.

Mandy Finds Myrtle's Bear

Mandy threw her schoolbag onto her bed and went into the kitchen.

"Did you have a nice day Dear? There's cake in the tin," her mother called out.

"Yes," said Mandy, opening the tin and taking out a slice. She munched cake as she wandered outside and meandered over to the pot-garden to look at the snails. But before she got there, something lying on the patio between two terracotta pots caught her eye. It was Myrtle's bear. He had been on a big adventure since falling out of Baxter, and he did not look like a prize-winning bear anymore.

147

The Britwhistles Win a Prize

"What's this?" Mandy said picking up the bear.

Wendy Hamilton

Mud covered him, his eyes were missing, his cardigan was full of holes, and he had lost Myrtle's precious blue ribbon. Mandy stooped and picked him up.

"What's this? Poor old bear, you look all banged up. You're dirty and blind, you poor thing. I wonder how you got here?"

"Look what I found, Mum!" she shouted as she ran into the house.

"What's that grubby old thing?" said Sandra, wrinkling her nose. "It smells like wet dog."

"It's a Teddy bear. I found him by the tomatoes. He's lost his eyes and one of his legs is wobbly. Do you think you could fix him?"

"I suppose so." Her mother took the bear and examined him. "But before I do anything, he is going in the wash. I've got a small load that needs doing." She walked into the laundry and popped him into the washing machine.

Mandy parked herself in front of the round window and watched the bear turn into a blur of red and brown. At the end of the cycle, she squeezed the catch of the door and pulled him out. He smelled of wildflowers and the colour of his fur and cardigan looked several shades lighter. Mandy skipped into the living room and held him out to her mother.

"He's all clean."

The Britwhistles Win a Prize

"That's much better," said Sandra, squeezing him. "It's too late in the day to dry him on the clothesline. I'll pop him in the dryer."

"That will take so long," said Mandy impatiently.

"Don't you have homework to do?"

"Yes," said Mandy, sighing. She dragged her feet slowly into her room and unzipped her school bag reluctantly. "I hate homework!"

Her mother remembered how much she hated homework as a child. "I'll make a deal with you," she said. "If you do your work and play with your brother nicely until bedtime, your bear will be as good as new in the morning. Is it a deal?"

"Ooh yes," shouted Mandy, pulling out her spelling book quickly.

As her mother promised, the bear was fixed by morning. She had exaggerated a little, however, when she said he would be as good as new. Nobody would give this tatty looking bear a blue ribbon. But his cardigan, though full of darns, was red again and his leg didn't wobble.

Sandra looked at her daughter anxiously, "I hope you don't mind his eyes; I couldn't find two matching buttons."

"I like them, it makes him look roguish and jolly. Thank you, thank you, Mum, I love him," sang Mandy, twirling around the house holding her bear out by his arms.

"Sit down and eat your breakfast or you will be late for school," laughed Sandra, thinking Mandy's reaction was worth the late night.

"I'm going to take him to school with me," said Mandy, propping the bear by her plate before shovelling cornflakes into her mouth.

"Slow down, you're eating like a pig," admonished her mother, spreading vegemite onto toast.

"I can't slow down; Jane will be here any moment." Even as she said it, the doorbell rang. "Got to go," she said, throwing down her spoon.

"Take this and eat it on the way," her mother said, passing her the toast.

"Thanks, Mum," said Mandy pulling on her backpack.

"And don't stop at the park after school, come straight home, I want to go through your old toys for the jumble sale. I want it all sorted out before your father gets home tomorrow.

"OK" yelled Mandy over her shoulder as she rushed out the door.

"Hi Jane, look what I found yesterday," said Mandy as the two girls walked down the front path. "Isn't he cool?"

"Hmm," said Jane politely. She was not into

bears. If she was going to have one, she would at least like a new one. She did not want to hurt her friend, however. "He reminds me a bit of that bear you liked at the show."

"Oh no," said Mandy. "That one was really cute, but this one is much better."

"What time does your father get home tomorrow?" Jane asked, changing the subject.

Mandy gave a little twirl and skip. "After lunch and I can't wait."

"I wonder what he's bringing you this time?" said Jane, thinking it would be something much nicer than the old bear her friend was so keen on.

"I don't know. He won't even give me a hint. It's going to take forever to get through today and tomorrow morning," said Mandy, sighing.

"I wish my father would go away more often," said Jane enviously, "then I might get fancy presents when he comes home like you do."

"You wouldn't like it," said Mandy, shaking her head, "you're lucky having your father around all the time. The best present in the world is not worth having him away for a long time."

Mandy kicked a stone and they walked for a distance in awkward silence.

"Do you want to play at the playground tonight?" said Jane at last.

"I can't."

"Why not, it's Friday night? We have the whole weekend for homework."

"Mum said I can't. She wants me to sort through my old toys for the jumble sale."

"My mother got me to do that the other night," said Jane sympathetically. "It was a real pain."

"A real pain, that's exactly what it is," said Mandy, "I'm not looking forward to this afternoon."

The Perfect Card and a Gift for Nelly

The time to send the Christmas invitation had rolled around again. Myrtle and Alfred stood in Molly's shop looking at the cards.

"What about this one?" said Alfred, pointing to a card with a goofy jester on the front.

"No, it's too much like the clown cards. There is no point wasting another year with clowns."

Alfred's face drooped. "You're right, they didn't work."

Myrtle picked out a card and smiled, "these puppies are adorable."

"Yes, and we haven't tried puppies," said Alfred, his face brightening.

154

Myrtle opened the card, scanned the inside and slapped it shut. "No good, it says 'get well soon.'"

"Hey Myrtle, look at this one, what about rabbits?"

"We've already done rabbits."

"We've done most things," said Alfred, sighing. "We've done a gipsy caravan, a donkey, a country scene and a seaside picture."

"Oh, Alfred, where are we going wrong, why won't they come?"

Alfred hung his head. "I don't know."

Molly, who had been watching, called: "Alfred and Myrtle, I've just received a new shipment of stock and something came I think you might like. I'll get it for you to look at. I won't be a tick."

The Britwhistles, full of curiosity, walked over to the counter while Molly nipped through the red curtain under the 'private' sign. As she promised she was back almost immediately.

"Do you like this one?" she asked, sliding a card across the counter to them.

Myrtle's eyes grew round as she looked at it. "It's perfect," she nodded.

"Shells and fish and big stripy lollypops, it couldn't be better," said Alfred, beaming.

Myrtle turned the front cover over and read aloud; "we could have fun in the sun if you come."

The Britwhistles Win a Prize

"That settles it," said Alfred, taking his wallet out of his pocket and sliding a five-dollar note across to Molly, "this is the card for us."

"You're right, Alfred," said Myrtle, her eyes shining, "the card's a sign that this year will be different. Now let's see if we can find something thin to pop inside it."

Alfred nodded and was about to follow her to the children's aisle, when Molly leaned forward and caught his arm.

"I saw something in the latest catalogue I think you might be interested in," she said, with a wink.

Alfred turned his head and called to Myrtle, "I'll be with you in a moment, Love."

Molly bent down and pulled a glossy brochure out from under the counter and leafed through the pages. "I was thinking you might like to give this to Nelly for Christmas," she whispered, swivelling it around and stabbing her finger on an advertisement.

Alfred gave a long, low whistle of delight. "Skunk Vesuvius, that sure is the granddaddy of all stink bombs. As you say, it is the perfect gift for Nelly."

"I'll have to order it in if you want it, I can't stock them, they're too potent to sell to schoolboys." Molly sighed. "It's a pity though, they would sell like hotcakes."

"What do they look like?" whispered Alfred, peering at the catalogue, "I can only see the box they're delivered in."

Molly looked around furtively and leaned forward. "That's exactly what they look like, a plain cardboard carton, that is the beauty of them, nobody suspects they are setting off a stink bomb when they open them up. You can even get one sent to Nelly through the post for two dollars extra."

Alfred's face lit up. "She wouldn't suspect a thing if it came through the post."

Molly chuckled and wiggled her eyebrows up and down. "You're right, she wouldn't." She slipped a form across the counter to Alfred. "Fill this out with Nelly's address and the date you want it to arrive."

"She'll guess it's a practical joke if she sees my name," said Alfred, frowning at the box under the word 'Sender.'

"You don't have to put your address on it, you can put the name of the company instead. Arcady Products sounds like shampoo."

"Wouldn't she wonder why they are sending her something she didn't order?"

"They've got that covered, there's a packing slip that says, 'you have won a free gift from our product range.'"

The Britwhistles Win a Prize

"Brilliant!" Alfred took a pen from his shirt pocket and filled out the form. He had barely finished when Myrtle called:

"Alfred, come and look at these."

"Coming," Alfred called back, as he paid Molly hastily.

"What do you think of this," said Myrtle, when he arrived. She handed him a flat beetle made of tin.

"I used to love these things when I was a boy," Alfred beamed. He squashed the metal flap behind the beetle rapidly and a series of clicks sounded. "I'm sure Peter would love one."

"I think Sally would too," said Myrtle, "and they are not too thick to slip in an envelope."

It took a long time to pick the right ones because there were so many to choose from, but they found the right ones at last. That afternoon Myrtle wrote the invitation with her best ink pen and her most handsome writing. "I'm sure this year will be different," she said as she licked the flap of the envelope and stuck it down firmly.

"I'm sure you are right," said Alfred.

Then they went to the Post office, bought a stamp, and dropped it into the post-box with high hopes.

Wendy Hamilton

Harry Bloomingdale Returns Home

When Mandy got home a surprise awaited her. In the covered area out the back were two large crates with foreign words stamped on them.

"What are those Mum?" she said, dropping her bag by the potted ferns and walking around them.

"They're a present from your father," her mother said, putting a hammer on the barbeque. "They've come early."

Mandy jumped up and down in excitement. "Oh boy oh boy, can we open them now?"

Sandra gave a little laugh. "No, a note came

159

with them that said we have to wait until he comes home, then we can open them together."

Mandy stopped bouncing and peered through the slits between the boards of the crates, but all she could see was straw. "This makes it even harder to wait for Dad to come home."

"I have something to make the time pass more quickly," her mother said, holding up two bags. "I want you to go through all your stuff. Broken things go in here," she lifted up a bag marked rubbish, "and stuff for the rummage sale goes in here," she lifted the other bag with jumble written on it.

"Aw do I have too?"

"You won't be opening these crates until it's done, even if your father is home," her mother said, firmly.

Mandy sighed, grabbed the bags and trailed off to her room. It was boring sorting through all the junk, but by bedtime Mandy had divided the pile into three. She put her new bear on top of the toys she was keeping and twisted the top of each bag into a knot.

"Good job," her mother said, as she tucked Mandy into bed. "We'll finish this tomorrow morning before Dad gets home."

"Will he be on the plane by now?"

"Yes. Every minute you are asleep he will be a

few miles closer."

"I don't think I will be able to sleep," said Mandy, snuggling down into her pillow.

"Well, just lie there quietly and think about him getting closer," her mother said, kissing her goodnight.

Morning was upon Mandy before she knew it. After a hurried breakfast, there was a frenzy of cleaning so the house would be nice for Dad coming home. At last, the dishes were done and the beds made. Apart from the pencil shavings and cookie crumbs on her floor, Mandy's room looked clean and tidy.

"Take this pile of clothes and put them in the entry with the bags for the jumble sale," said Sandra, giving her daughter a stack of Billy's outgrown clothes. "I'll vacuum your room and then we will be finished."

"Ok Mum," said Mandy, perching Myrtle's bear on top of the stretch-n-grows. She cantered into the front entrance, pretending the bear was riding a horse. A movement caught her eye through the glass of the door. Without thinking, she dumped everything on the hall table and ran to open it.

"A taxi's here, Dad's home!" she yelled, hurtling down the front path and into her father's arms.

"Wooo, you nearly knocked me over, Mandy-

The Britwhistles Win a Prize

Pandy," he said, swinging her high into the air. He put her down as her mother came hurrying along the path carrying Billy on her hip.

"Harry, your early," said Sandra looking pleased.

"I got an earlier flight," he said, kissing her. "And who is this big boy?" he asked, ruffling Billy's hair.

Billy took his thumb out of his mouth, "Billy," he said solemnly.

"No, this can't be the Billy I left behind," his father said, his eyebrows shooting up.

"Yesss, I am," said Billy, thrilled to be big.

"Yes, it is," said Mandy.

"Well, if you say so, I'll have to believe it," he said, taking Billy from his wife and swinging him around like an aeroplane before putting him down. "You two can help me carry my things in." He pointed to some luggage by the gate. "And then who is ready to open a present?"

There was a flurry of activity and soon the Bloomingdale family were gathered around the biggest crate. Harry picked the hammer off the barbeque and prised it apart. Then everyone pulled the straw away.

"Wow, is it a merry-go-round horse?" said Mandy, looking at the brightly painted wooden horse.

"Better than that," her father said, levering the

162

top off the second crate. He reached down and pulled out a fist full of railway tracks. "Merry-go-round horses just go around and around in a circle. There are two-hundred-and-fifty tracks in here and this horse can go anywhere you lay them down."

"Wow," said Mandy again. "How do you make it go?"

"It's clockwork," her father said, rescuing an enormous key from Billy, who was using it to dig up the potted ferns, "you wind it up and it runs along the track on these." He gently kicked the set of wheels under the horse.

They spent a wonderful morning laying a track all around the back of the yard, up to the big fig tree at the top of the hill and back again. Then while Harry told Sandra about his travels, Mandy and Billy took it in turns to ride the horse until lunchtime. It was disappointing when the rain started.

"Cheer up Mandy, it's not as bad as you think," her father said, pulling two small packages from his pocket, "I was saving these for a rainy day and now you can have them." He handed one to her and one to Billy.

In Billy's package was a small car, but Mandy's present was a wooden tube with four nails sticking out of the end.

"What is it?" said Mandy

The Britwhistles Win a Prize

"It's a French knitting set," her father said, "I picked it up in Paris for you. The instructions are in the middle of it."

Mandy turning it around saw a little wad of paper jammed inside the tube. She pulled it out with her fingernails and unfolded it.

Her mother rummaged in her knitting bag and took out a ball of bright red wool. "You might like to start with this," she said, handing it to Mandy before disappearing into the kitchen.

The doorbell rang.

"Can you get that Harry?" called Sandra, lifting a leg of lamb into a roasting pan, "it will be the lady collecting the jumble sale stuff."

"OK Honey." He opened the door.

Mandy sitting in the living room heard the

doorbell and a murmur of voices in the entrance, but she took no notice. She was too busy trying to wind the wool around the nails the proper way.

"Is this all of it?" Harry called to his wife.

"Yes, apart from the pile on the hall table," she called back, as she popped the meat into the oven.

With one swoop Harry dumped the clothes and Mandy's bear into an open bag and twisted the top into a knot. "Here we go," he said to Mrs Grundy. "I'll help you carry these out to your car.

A Terrible Truth

There were few things Myrtle enjoyed more than a 'jolly good clear out,' and there was no better excuse than the annual jumble sale. She hummed as she worked and occasionally spoke her thoughts out loud to objects in the room. This morning, like the Bloomingdales, she had two rubbish sacks, one marked 'rubbish,' and the other 'jumble sale.' Every drawer of the large chest in the front bedroom was open, and Myrtle was sorting through the stuff in them. She pulled a man's sweater from the bottom drawer, held it up and considered it with a tilted head and narrowed eyes.

"That can go," she said to the braided rug. "He'll never wear that again. I need locks fitted on

166

the fridge and cake tins." Her head straightened as she folded it and put it in the jumble-sale-bag. She dug into the bottom of the drawer and pulled out a hair clip.

"Wrong colour, what was I thinking buying an orange bow?" She was about to put it in the jumble bag when she saw the clip was broken. "Rubbish," she said to the candlestick. She threw it into the other bag with a smile of satisfaction. Then, whistling softly, she delved into the far back of the drawer and pulled out a shoebox.

"Oh my," she said. Her face turned white and her brisk energy evaporated. She stared at the box for some time before slowly opening the lid and lifting out a bundle of large Christmas cards. She gently untied the purple ribbon and lifted the first card from the pile and opened it with a sigh.

Something was bothering Myrtle, but she did not tell the braided rug or the candlestick about it, it was too painful for that. The only sound was the clock ticking as Myrtle silently read the line of regret scrawled inside. When she finished, she closed it softly and stared listlessly at the beamed ceiling. The shell and fish card they had pinned so many hopes on, had yielded nothing so far, and she knew in her heart this Christmas would come and go like all the others. Peter and Sally would open their

167

The Britwhistles Win a Prize

presents far away, and she and Alfred would eat ham and plum pudding alone in their quiet house. It made her sad to think they had missed another year of seeing their grandchildren grow. She spread the cards out like a fan and counted them one by one. When she had finished counting, a truly dreadful thought hit her. So dreadful she dropped the cards and hobbled out of the house and into the garden. "Alfred, stop digging and listen to me," she said in a shaky voice.

"I'm listening, Myrtle," said Alfred, leaning on the handle of his spade.

"How old do you think Peter and Sally are now?"

"Oh, I don't know, I always think of them as about six or seven."

"Me too, because that is when we last saw them. However, I have been doing some calculations. It is over ten years since we last saw them, so they must be sixteen and seventeen or more….. almost grown-up."

"Almost grown up," Alfred echoed. He was so shocked that he sat down in his wheelbarrow without realizing it was full of manure.

"They will be too old to want toy bears," said Myrtle, sitting down on the heap beside him. "Or traffic light tongues, or seashells and fairy-tale beds."

Wendy Hamilton

We have missed our grandchildren's childhood.

The Britwhistles Win a Prize

"They may still want to go fishing," said Alfred, brightening.

"But not with an old woman in a sailor suit and an old man wearing hooks in the brim of his hat."

"You are right," he said, deflating again.

We have missed our grandchildren's childhood. Both thought it, though neither spoke aloud. To speak aloud would have made the horrible truth seem even worse. Instead, they silently put an arm around each other. They sat there much longer than five minutes, and neither of them even thought to look at a watch. A frozen chicken truck drove by, but they did not notice the rumbling. They did not even notice the damp from the manure seeping into their clothes; at least not for some time. Wet underpants, however, have a way of getting the most distracted person's attention.

"Yuck! Fancy sitting all this time in goat poop," said Myrtle, disgusted at the state of the back of her dress. "Come inside and get cleaned up Dear, then we will have lunch."

"I don't feel like eating," said Alfred, flicking squashed droppings off his trousers as best he could.

"Neither do I," said Myrtle. "We will have a cup of tea instead."

And together they walked slowly up the path, holding hands. They looked tired and frail, suddenly.

Wendy Hamilton

The Church Fair

With the excitement of her father coming home, Mandy forgot all about her bear. It was several days before she noticed he was missing, and by then nobody thought to connect his disappearance with the jumble bags.

"I don't know? It's a mystery," said Sandra to her husband later that evening when the children were in bed. "I've looked everywhere. You haven't seen a small bear anywhere, have you, Harry?"

"Not me," he shrugged, never giving the tatty toy he shoved into the jumble bag a thought.

By the day of the fair Mandy's bear was still missing. Although they could have walked to the church the Bloomingdales took their car, because

171

The Britwhistles Win a Prize

they hoped to snag too many bargains to carry. As they pulled into the church car park, Sandra opened her handbag and swivelled around. "Here you go Sweetheart," she said, poking her arm through the gap in the front seats, "have fun with this," she handed Mandy a five-dollar note.

Mandy's eyes grew round. Even one dollar went a long way at a church fair. "Thanks Mum," she said, putting it in the little beaded purse she held.

Her father twisted around, "meet us back at the car in two hours."

Mandy nodded, opened the door and got out.

"If you get lost, go to the church office," her mother called after her.

"I won't get lost. See you later."

Mandy skipped across the front lawn of the church. Although she went there every Sunday, the grounds covered in fairground equipment looked very different. There was a Ferris wheel, a merry-go-round, dodgem cars, and a blow-up bouncy castle. Next to the graveyard, Molly was selling pony rides to small children, while in the paddock by the car park Wilbur supervised the motorbike rides. Children were dipping for plastic fish in a booth beside the caravan selling hotdogs and candyfloss, and a clown wandered about with a big bunch of helium balloons. Nothing, however, was as popular as the dunking booth. Half the school was queuing for the chance to dunk Mr Nugent. Among them was Jane. Mandy ran towards her, waving. "Hi Jane," she yelled.

"Hi Mandy," said Jane, as her friend skidded to a halt beside her. "Do you want to have a go at sinking Mr Nugent?"

"No," said Mandy. "I don't want to waste a dollar, I'm not a good shot."

"That man is," giggled Jane, as Alfred hit a bullseye and Mr Nugent fell with a shout into the barrel of water.

"Do you want to come with me to the jumble sale?" asked Mandy, "you need to get in early if you want the good stuff."

"No, you go on ahead," said Jane, "I don't want to lose my place in line. I'll meet up with you later."

"OK," said Mandy, waving goodbye.

The church hall was just as transformed as the yard outside. Mounds of used clothing or books covered trestle tables, and the produce table by the tea servery sagged under big pumpkins and long marrows. The most interesting stall by far was the White Elephant table, yet all the women who clustered so thickly around the other stalls, kept well away from it. A woman stood looking at a lampstand but that was all.

The Britwhistles Win a Prize

Myrtle at Nelly's bric-a-brac table.

Wendy Hamilton

"Have you found anything exciting?" Mandy asked, sidling up to her mother.

"I haven't had a chance," that ghastly woman, Nelly, is in charge of the White Elephant stall.

"Can I go and have a look?"

"Great idea, you won't have any problems. Have fun, but make sure you come back and tell me if you see anything I would like."

"OK," promised Mandy scooting off.

There was lots of bric-a-brac on the trestle table. Mandy glanced over the pile without much interest. A pair of roller skates and a Barbie horse held her attention; until she noticed the left boot was missing a wheel, and the horse had a broken leg.

"Games and toys down there," said Nelly to Mandy bossily. She turned back to Myrtle who stood with her hand on the lampstand.

"Like I was saying," said Nelly, "that Roger is a real villain, the way he up and left Leanne. They were only married for eight episodes. I knew he was a baddie when he first walked on the screen because he had polished shoes."

Myrtle's expression was wooden and her eyes glazed. While she was searching about for a way of escape, Mandy was digging through a cardboard box under the table. Suddenly Mandy found something that made her heart leap. From underneath a broken lamp, a pair of mismatched eyes stared at her pleadingly. She pulled her bear out, clutched him to her heart and went straight over to Nelly.

"Please, this is my bear," she said excitedly. "He got lost and we couldn't find him anywhere."

"A likely story," said Nelly, in a tone that implied she did not think it likely at all. "You can't just take things. You'll have to pay for it."

"How much is he?"

Nelly was about to say fifty cents when Mandy said:

"Would five dollars be enough?"

"That will do," said Nelly, snatching the money quickly.

"That must be a very special bear," said Myrtle, seizing her opportunity to walk away with Mandy. She liked the small girl with freckles and pigtails. She reminded her a little of Sally.

"Oh, he is," said Mandy with a serious expression. "I found him one day outside by the tomato plants. He was all dirty and had no eyes. Mummy washed him and fixed him, and I was so sad when he got lost."

"Can I meet him?" asked Myrtle, smiling at the small girl's earnestness.

"Of course," said Mandy, turning him around to face his maker.

"Oh my!" said Myrtle, sucking in her breath sharply. "I know this bear."

"You do?"

"Yes. I made him. I won first prize with him, and then I lost him. He used to have little black bead eyes and a lovely blue ribbon pinned to his cardigan. Right here," she said, poking his chest.

This was startling information.

Mandy looked at the bear... then she looked at the nice old lady...she looked back to her precious bear...then back at the nice old lady. Suddenly she made up her mind.

"Do you want him back?" she asked bravely.

"It would not be right to take him from you," said Myrtle, dabbing the corners of her eyes with her handkerchief. "I can tell he wants to belong to you. He looks so happy. When he lived with me, he looked sad."

"Thank you very much," said Mandy, hugging him with relief.

"Are your parents here Dear, I'd like to meet them if they are?" asked Myrtle, thinking what a lovely polite little girl she was.

"Yes, this is my mother," said Mandy as Sandra came over to see who her daughter was talking to.

"Hello, I'm Myrtle Britwhistle," said Myrtle, smiling at Sandra.

The Britwhistles Win a Prize

"I'm Sandra Bloomingdale," said Sandra, smiling back.

"She's the lady who made my bear, and she says I can keep him," broke in Mandy, doing little jumps on the spot.

"Are you sure it's alright for her to keep the bear?"

"Absolutely," said Myrtle firmly.

"Then you've made someone very happy Mrs Britwhistle," smiled Sandra, stroking Mandy's head. "This is my husband Harry and our son Billy," she added, as they entered the room and came over.

"Call me Myrtle. That's my husband Alfred, over there," she admitted, sighing, as she pointed to Alfred Henry sneaking up behind Nelly.

"He's not really going to shoot her with that bow and arrow, is he?" asked Sandra, stifling laughter.

"Very likely, I'm just happy it's a toy and won't do any damage."

There was a great howl as the suckered end of the arrow hit the broad target of Nelly's bottom. She turned, and when she saw it was Alfred, she left her table and ran at him. Alfred threw the bow into the air and fled; for a podgy man he was surprisingly quick on his feet. He ran out the front door with Nelly chasing him and they both disappeared into the crowd outside.

"I'm so embarrassed," said Myrtle, turning red. "He's a terrible tease when he's in the mood."

"Don't be," said Sandra. "By the look of all the people flocking to that stall now she's gone, I think there are many people who are happy about it."

"That is a very nice thing to say," said Myrtle, looking less flushed. "Do you live locally?"

"Yes, over in Wollondilly."

"That is just behind where we live. Have you lived there long?"

"We've been here about two years," said Sandra. She looked into Myrtle's kind face and took a risk, "but we haven't made many friends yet."

Myrtle's whole heart went out to her, and she also took a risk. "Do you have family coming for Christmas?" she asked.

"No," sighed Sandra, "it's just us four."

"Would you like to come to our house and share Christmas with us?" Myrtle stumbled over her words in her eagerness to get them out.

"Oh, I wasn't meaning to make it your problem," said Sandra, embarrassed.

"You didn't," Myrtle assured her. "I was thinking it would solve a problem for us. Alfred and I would love to have young people about the house on Christmas day. It doesn't seem special with only the two of us and the cat."

The Britwhistles Win a Prize

"Can we Mum, can we, please can we," pleaded Mandy starting to bounce up and down again.

"Well if you really mean it?" hesitated Sandra, "what do you say Harry?"

"I would love to spend Christmas in the company of a man so skilful with a bow and arrow," said Harry with a twinkle in his eye.

"Now that's settled," said Myrtle beaming, "there is no need to wait until Christmas for our first visit together. How about coming for lunch after church tomorrow?"

"I would like that very much," said Sandra. "What's your address?"

"Three Station Road," replied Myrtle, as they all walked towards the crowded White Elephant stall.

Wendy Hamilton

The Best Prize of All

It was Christmas Day and delicious smells were wafting out of the Britwhistles little wooden house. In the oven of the big woodstove a large ham was baking, and on the hob a plum pudding tied in a cloth bubbled in a pot of water. Above them, the annual Large-Card and Christmas-Greetings from the cat sat on the mantelpiece, while over the top of every doorframe were branches of pine, holly berries, and tartan bows. In the front room stood an extra-large Christmas tree, but the box for Myrtle and the package for Alfred were not under it because they were hidden away in a red sack among lots of brightly wrapped parcels.

The kitchen door opened and Alfred came in carrying a bucket of new potatoes and a bowl of fat yellow plums. "I got the potatoes and plums from the garden and I brought you in a bit of mint while I was at it," he said, holding up a sprig of mint.

"Good," said Myrtle, opening the oven door and lifting out the ham. "Could you scrub those spuds and put them on for me Alfred, while I finish this?"

"Right oh," said Alfred, tipping them in the sink.

Alfred cleaned the potatoes and popped them in a pot while Myrtle stuck cherries on the ham with toothpicks. Then there were peas to shell, cream to whip, and a pavlova to top with cream and strawberries. Alfred whistled 'Rudolph the Red-Nosed Reindeer' as he worked while Myrtle hummed 'Away in a Manger,' and by the time the morning was getting late the kitchen table was loaded with good things to eat.

"There, we are all ready," said Myrtle, untying her apron and hanging it on the back of the pantry door. "Time to get tidied up."

She went into the front bedroom and put on her red dress with green spots.

"Do you want me in the Santa Suit?" said Alfred, as he hunted in the closet for his reindeer antlers.

Wendy Hamilton

A Wonderul Christmas.

The Britwhistles Win a Prize

"Not yet, wait until they arrive, I'll gather everyone around the Christmas tree, and while I'm doing that you slip out and pull it on."

Myrtle had barely finished speaking when the doorbell tinkled.

"They're here," she said excitedly.

Alfred, seeing the antlers, hurriedly grabbed them and rammed the headband onto his head before bustling to the door and flinging it open.

"Come in, come in," he cried, as his face crinkled into a wide smile.

Then people and hugs, laughter and Merry Christmases filled the room.

"I made you a card Tooty," said Billy, handing Alfred a rumpled card with two rectangles and four circles on it. "I drew Lulu because we always play in her when we come here."

"And I made one for you, Britty," said Mandy, passing Myrtle a card. "I drew my bear because without him we might never have met you and Tooty."

Sandra looked flustered. "I hope you don't mind them calling you that, Myrtle, they made up the names themselves. Mr and Mrs Britwhistle, does sound rather formal."

"Tooty! I like that name," said Alfred, beaming. "Toot toot," he said, pretending to pull an imaginary train-whistle.

"And I like Britty," said Myrtle, "it's a nice friendly name." She opened the card and read, 'Happy Christmas Britty, I can't wait to stay the holidays with you. Love from Mandy.' Myrtle's glasses suddenly went misty. "There is only one place good enough for these beautiful cards," she said. And taking the Large-Card off the mantelpiece, she put Mandy and Billy's cards on either side of the cat's card.

Then she nodded at Alfred and Alfred, nodding back, quietly crept from the room.

"If you come with me children," said Myrtle, when he had gone, "I think we might be about to have a special visitor." She led the way over to the Christmas tree and called:

"Santa are you ready?"

At the name of Santa, Billy's eyes grew very round.

There was no answer so Myrtle said, "if we count to a hundred, I think Santa will visit us."

So, with much laughing and shouting, the Bloomingdales counted. And while they counted, Myrtle slipped the Large-Card into her scrapbooking box. Then at the exact moment they chanted "one-hundred," Santa bounced into the room, dragging his red sack with him.

The Britwhistles Win a Prize

"Ho-ho-ho," he said cheerfully, "what do I have here?" He reached into his bag and pulled out a lumpy package and a gold and silver striped box. "Here you go, Billy," he said, handing him the lumpy package. He gave the box to Mandy. "Merry Christmas, Mandy."

Mandy untied the gold ribbon wrapped around it, carefully opened the lid, and lifted out a little blue sweater.

"I thought your bear might like more clothes, so I made him a whole new wardrobe," said Myrtle, looking at Mandy as she helped Billy open his parcel.

"Thank you thank you Britty," said Mandy rushing over to hug her.

"And now Billy has a friend to keep your bear company," said Myrtle, as her second-best bear fell out of the wrapping paper.

But Santa had not finished yet. There was a long thin packet for Billy and a squat round one for Mandy.

"A fishing rod," squealed Billy, waving it about happily.

"A red shell bucket," said Mandy, pleased.

Then there were olives and nuts and pickled onions and fancy cheeses for the adults and of course, a new teapot for Myrtle and socks for Alfred.

Then Alfred took off his Santa suit and Mandy and Billy gave the Britwhistles a packet each.

In Myrtle's packet was a coil of French knitting that rose in a shallow cup shape.

"It's for your teapot to sit on. It's the first thing I've ever knitted and I made it for you," said Mandy, a puzzled expression crossed her face, "it's supposed to be flat though, I don't know what went wrong."

"It doesn't matter a bit," said Myrtle, hugging her, "this is the nicest gift of the day, thank you so much."

"I didn't make your present, Tooty," said Billy, I found it by the frog pond."

Alfred unwrapped a smooth stone and whistled with delight. "You don't often find a stone with a hole through the middle of it." He took a length of string from his pocket, threaded it through the hole and tied the ends into a knot. "Now I will show you something special," he said, twirling it.

Myrtle twisted her head and looked at the clock on the wall. "Oh, my goodness," she gasped, laying her hand on Alfred's arm, "not now Love, the taxi will be here before we have finished lunch if we don't get started."

Alfred stopped twirling the stone and put it in his pocket, "I'll show you after lunch Billy, we can't have your parent's missing their cruise."

"Come and eat everyone," said Myrtle, leading the way into the kitchen.

Everyone sat around the laden table and held hands while Alfred gave thanks to God for friends and food, then they ate and drank, laughed and pulled Christmas crackers, and were very merry until everyone was so full that they couldn't eat another bite.

Finally, Harry looked at his watch and pushed back his chair. "Thank you so much Alfred and Myrtle, for making this such a happy Christmas," he said, "Sandra and the children and I can't thank you enough."

"Think nothing of it," said Alfred, gruffly as he straightened his paper crown, "it is our pleasure."

"It certainly is," said Myrtle, stroking Billy's hair, "you can't imagine how much we are looking forward to having the children stay with us."

After this they all fell silent and everyone was on the brink of getting a bit sentimental and teary, when the honk of the taxi horn saved them from awkwardness. Then it was back to laughing as they said their goodbyes, and after they had waved until the taxi was out of sight, the Britwhistles and the children had the whole afternoon before them for party games and fun.

That night, Alfred carried a sleepy boy up the stairs and laid him in the bed under the Peter-cross-stitch, while Myrtle helped Mandy into the bed beneath Sally's name. Then they tiptoed down the stairs and climbed into their old-fashioned iron bed.

The cuckoo clock started to chime as Myrtle put her teapot-stand beside the candlestick and Alfred put his pebble next to the fly spray. Then the only sounds were the wind in the trees and the cuckoo's repetitive little who-who while they read their bibles. Eventually, they were finished and Myrtle blew out the candle.

As usual, Alfred was the first to speak.

"Listen to that Myrtle."

"What?" said Myrtle. She said it a little absent-mindedly, however, because she was thinking happy thoughts about Mandy's gift.

But instead of saying "silence, no electronic buzzing," he said, "little snores."

Myrtle shifted her mind off her teapot-stand. "So they are," she said with genuine amazement, "what a lovely noise!"

"I think this is the most interesting rock I've ever seen." Alfred's voice hovered in the darkness. "That was very generous of Billy to give it to me. You seldom find them with a hole in the middle like this one has. I think the best part of the afternoon was

189

when we twirled it round and round," he chuckled. "Did you see Billy's eyes when he heard the buzzing noise it made? They almost popped out."

"The best part for me was when Mandy and I got all my teapots out of the cupboard and sat them on her teapot-stand one by one," said Myrtle happily, her words floating up to meet his. "Perhaps we should go to the beach tomorrow?"

"I'd like that," said Alfred, sitting upright.

"You two could fish while Sally and I collect shells," continued Myrtle.

"Then we could all have a traffic light ice cream," said Alfred dreamily as he lay back down again.

They were both silent for a while, dwelling on pleasant things. Alfred visualised hideous tongues, while his wife imagined cockle and scallop shells. Finally, just as Myrtle was about to say, "I think I will wear my sailor suit tomorrow," the cricket chirped.

"There's that beastly cricket again," fussed Alfred, whisking out of bed before Myrtle could light the candle. There was a thump as he fell over his slippers and landed on the floor.

"Oh Alfred, Honey," said Myrtle, striking a match, "you will wake the children! Couldn't you leave the poor little cricket alone for one night?

It's a lovely sound."

Myrtle peeped in at Mandy asleep in bed.

The Britwhistles Win a Prize

"It's annoying," said Alfred, wrenching up the window, "and tonight is the night I will finally get him."

"Quietly Alfred," said Myrtle in a loud stage whisper.

Alfred did not answer. He leaned out the window and sprayed the underneath of the sill vigorously.

Myrtle touched the match to the candle and the flame caught hold of the wick. "I think I'll go upstairs and check that Mandy and Billy are alright."

"Good idea, Myrtle, take the candle with you, I won't need the light."

When she had gone, Alfred leant as far out of the window as he dared and squinted at Nelly's porch. He could see by the light of the moon, a large package next to the backdoor. Good, he thought, the stink bomb is there. He slid the window down slowly and climbed back into bed, chuckling. "Nelly will get a surprise when she opens it," he said to Marmaduke, who was lying by his feet. "Perhaps Molly might even smell it from her place if the wind is right."

Myrtle, blissfully unaware of Alfred's 'gift,' mounted the stairs. First, she peeped into Peter's room. The little fishing rod leaned against the knob of the bed and Billy lay under the blue and yellow quilt, fast asleep. Myrtle pulled the cover up a little before hobbling across the landing and into Sally's room. Mandy was also asleep. Myrtle held the candle higher and saw her bear peeping out from under the red and green quilt. She smiled as she stared at the bear, and as she gazed, the bear nodded at her and the stitches of his mouth curved into a grin. Myrtle's hand flew to her mouth, "impossible," she whispered, taking off her glasses and rubbing her eyes, "it must be a trick of the light." She put her glasses on again and looked at the bear once more, but there was nothing unusual to see. Then she turned and tiptoed down the stairs.

"Are they alright?" asked Alfred, as she got back into bed.

"Sound asleep," said Myrtle, thumping her pillow and settling down comfortably.

"Good," said Alfred. He turned onto his side and dropped off to sleep like a pebble falling off a cliff.

Myrtle, however, lay awake for a long time thinking of the children and the prize-bear upstairs. Somehow it no longer mattered that she had lost her only blue ribbon, or that she was unlikely to win another. The real prize was the Bloomingdale family. Myrtle smiled in the dark as the cricket sang. Their friendship was worth more than a hundred blue ribbons.

About the Author

Wendy Hamilton comes from a small island nation on the bottom of the world called New Zealand. In case you don't know where that is, it is right of Australia and down a bit. Or rather, that is where it should be. Rude map makers often leave it off, which is almost as annoying as being an island under the P in Pacific Ocean.

Contrary to popular belief, people Down-Under do not hang off the globe upside down. Or if they do, they are not aware of it. Neither do they walk on their heads or wear grass skirts. They do however have volcanoes and earthquakes, so Wendy lives instead with her husband Ian and four grown children in Australia; the land of snakes, droughts and bush fires.

Wendy loves to make things and has hands that can beautify anything she touches. They cannot however, make a successful sponge cake and have never once managed to catch a ball.

When she was very small, Wendy's mother introduced her to the Public Library where there was a fascinating assortment of books and a wonderful old Grandfather clock. Wendy spent much of her childhood there, reading adventure stories and drawing flowers in her math's book. Thankfully algebra is long gone. The habit of reading and drawing remains however, and has multiplied into Wendy's own illustrated books.

Nowadays (when she is not riding in trains or cars), Wendy can be found in various libraries drawing and writing as she travels throughout New South Wales with Ian, as he goes about his job as a Research Scientist.

Other Books By Wendy Hamilton

Children's Novels

The Britwhistles and the Elasticizer
Little House in the Bush
Little House in the Cow Paddock

Children's Picture books

The Unlucky Snails
The Unlucky Snails go to France

These can be found at
www.zealauspublishing.com